# Trading Places

CLAUDIA MILLS

# Trading Places

FARRAR, STRAUS AND GIROUX
New York

## Author's Note

The Mini-Society program in this novel is inspired by the excellent Mini-Society curriculum created by Marilyn Kourilsky and used widely in elementary schools throughout America. Some liberties have been taken with the details of the curriculum for artistic purposes. This novel has not been authorized or endorsed by Marilyn Kourilsky or anyone else associated with the Mini-Society curriculum.

Copyright © 2006 by Claudia Mills
All rights reserved
Distributed in Canada by Douglas & McIntyre Ltd.
Printed in the United States of America
Designed by Barbara Grzeslo
First edition, 2006
1   3   5   7   9   10   8   6   4   2

www.fsgkidsbooks.com

Library of Congress Cataloging-in-Publication Data
Mills, Claudia.
    Trading places / Claudia Mills.— 1st ed.
      p.   cm.
    Summary: When fifth-grade twins, Amy and Todd, tackle a school project, they also have to cope with issues of friendship at school and problems at home, including their father's unemployment.
    ISBN-13: 978-0-374-31798-0
    ISBN-10: 0-374-31798-4
    [1. Self-perception—Fiction.   2. Family problems—Fiction.
3. Unemployment—Fiction.   4. Schools—Fiction.   5. Friendship—
Fiction.   6. Brothers and sisters—Fiction.   7. Twins—Fiction.]   I. Title.

PZ7.M63963 Tra 2006
[Fic]—dc22

                                                                    2005046371

*To all my friends
at the Children's Literature Festival
at Central Missouri State University
in Warrensburg*

# Trading Places

It was Monday morning of the first full week of school, and Todd Davidson's house was in its usual cheerful chaos—except for the empty place at the kitchen table where his father should have been, finishing up his quick breakfast of Grape-Nuts and coffee before heading off to work.

"Todd, I've put lunch money for you and Amy in your backpack, and the emergency contact forms, and the fifth-grade parent volunteer form," Todd's mother said, checking the list she had made for herself on the dry-erase board hanging by the telephone.

"You know how your sister is." She shot an affectionate glance at Amy, who was lost in a book, as always. She lowered her voice conspiratorially. "If I gave them to her, she'd write poems on the backs of the forms, and they'd end up lost in her desk along with notes from Kelsey and Julia, and who knows what else."

Todd grinned at his mother. On the third day of school, Amy's desk was already a disaster area.

Even though he and Amy were twins, they were as opposite in every other way as could be: Todd was tall, with curly dark hair; Amy was short, with straight fair hair. Todd was organized, and Amy was disorganized—as Todd knew all too well from being in the same class as Amy at Riverside Elementary School for the second year in a row. But Todd was glad that at his school twins could be together. Especially this year.

"Check," Todd told his mother. "What's in the sealed envelope?"

"That thing Ms. Ives wanted the parents to write."

"About Amy and me?"

Amy put down *A Little Princess*. Todd was sure she had read it half a dozen times already. "What did you say about us?"

"Oh, you know," their mother said, "the same old stuff. 'Todd loves to build things. Amy loves to write. Todd is the competitive one. Amy is the sensitive one.' "

"Did you say, 'Amy's desk is a black hole. Todd's desk is the neatest in the class'?" Todd teased.

Amy whacked him with her book, but not very hard, whether because she didn't want to hurt his shoulder or because she didn't want to damage her beloved book, Todd didn't know. Probably both.

"I couldn't say everything. I have to leave some surprises for Ms. Ives."

"Amy's desk is a surprise, all right."

"It isn't that messy!" Amy said.

Their mother looked at the clock. "Ten till eight. We'd better go. I told Max I'd be in early today to help with the inventory." Max was the store manager and their mother's boss. "Where's Dad?"

Amy and Todd exchanged a glance.

"Upstairs," Todd said, keeping his answer deliberately vague.

"Doing what?"

Todd saw Amy hesitate a split second before she replied, "Reading." When he had walked by the open door of their parents' bedroom ten minutes ago, his father had been lying on the unmade bed, still in his pajamas, staring up at the ceiling, while Wiggy, their fourteen-year-old sheepdog, dozed on the floor next to him.

"I hope he's reading the *Denver Post* job ads. I know the economy in Colorado is terrible right now, but he's not going to find a job by lying on the bed, staring at the ceiling."

So she did know.

"Okay, let's go. Bye, honey! Get some groceries! The list is on the fridge!" she called loudly, in the direction of the stairs.

If their father heard, he gave no answer.

· · ·

Todd's teacher, Ms. Ives, had decorated their classroom with a row of six-foot-high cardboard buildings—bank, school, hospital, library, shops—lined up against the far wall. These were for the Mini-Society the kids were going to create together in the first two months of fifth grade.

Todd's best friend, Isaiah Quinn, sat right next to the cardboard city, all the way across the room from Todd. Teachers had some secret way of finding out which kids were best friends and then assigning them desks as far apart as possible. But Todd and Isaiah had been best friends for so long that they didn't need to talk to each other to know what the other one was doing, or thinking, or feeling.

As the fifth graders took their chairs down from the tops of their desks, Todd heard one chair crash to the floor. He didn't have to turn around to know whose chair it was.

"Isaiah," Ms. Ives said. "That's a warning."

Todd knew that in another week she wouldn't be giving Isaiah warnings about falling furniture. She'd just sigh and look away.

After morning announcements, Ms. Ives put the daily math challenge problem on the overhead projector. Todd solved it easily, but most of the other kids needed the full ten minutes.

"Who has the answer to this one?"

Of course Isaiah waved his hand, and of course Isaiah got it wrong. In another week Ms. Ives wouldn't be calling on Isaiah first for the math challenge problem.

"Todd?"

He told her his answer.

"Good job, Todd!"

It was a new room and a new teacher, with a few different kids in the class. But for the most part everything was the same as always.

At school.

Not at home.

At home everything was horribly different.

Ms. Ives looked over at the board, where she had the daily schedule written out in her perfect cursive writing. She was the youngest teacher Todd had ever had. He had heard this was her first year of teaching.

"Class?" she said. Todd could tell she was nervous because she turned everything into a question. "Please get out your Mini-Society folders?"

Todd's folder was right on top of the other folders in his desk. Across the room, he saw Amy fumbling in her desk, searching for hers. He was pretty sure she had left it in her backpack, crammed together with a bunch of other folders, library books, and doodads for her hair.

Isaiah gave a whoop of glee as he found his. The lid of his desk banged down loudly. There was something wrong with the hinge, and Isaiah hadn't yet learned that he had to close the top gently.

Ms. Ives glared at him. "That's a second warning, Isaiah."

Amy raised her hand.

"Amy?"

"I can't find my folder."

Todd raised his hand.

"Todd?"

"It's in her backpack."

Amy grinned at him and ran to the coatrack to get it. Ms. Ives sighed. "All right, class? Do you all have your folders *now*?"

Everyone did, though crybaby Violet LaFarge, who sat next to Todd, looked ready to burst into tears as she tried to smooth out a tiny bent spot on one corner of her folder. And Isaiah's folder had slipped off his desk onto the floor. As he bent down to pick it up, his chair slid back into the chair of the kid next to him, who was absent that day. That chair tipped over, with another crash.

"It was an accident!" Isaiah called out.

Todd could tell Ms. Ives was debating what to do. She had already told the class she didn't give third warnings. You got two warnings, and then with the third offense you were sent to the office. No one had been sent to the office yet this year. Of course, it was only the third day of school.

Ms. Ives forced a smile. "Let's not have any more accidents."

As if it were that easy. Accidents happened. And they happened often to Isaiah.

"In the Mini-Society curriculum," Ms. Ives said, "we create our own society, right here in our classroom. We'll design a flag, and create a currency—that's our money—and all of you will get paid in that currency for the various classroom jobs that you do each week, like taking the attendance cards to the office and watering our plants. And together we'll make all the rules we're going to follow."

"Can we make a rule that we can chew gum?" one boy asked.

"No. Our Riverside Elementary rules will continue to apply."

"So what rules can we make?" Amy's best friend Julia Fuller asked.

"Rules about our classroom economy. For example, will we pay taxes on our earnings?"

"No!" another kid called out.

Ms. Ives smiled. Apparently she had been hoping this would be the response. "Ah, but taxes make it possible for us to fund various goods and services for our society, which otherwise we wouldn't be able to have. We'll come back to the question of taxes later. For now, I want you all to start thinking about the goods and services that *you* will be creating. You'll be selling these to your fellow Mini-Society members at our first selling session four weeks from today. And then you'll be selling to your families and the other fifth-grade classes at our 'international' selling session two weeks later."

Isaiah's hand was in the air now. Isaiah didn't wave just his hand, he waved his whole body. "Will we get paid real money for our goods and services?"

"No, you'll be paid in our Mini-Society money, but you'll be able to buy real things with it."

Isaiah's face brightened. He never had any money. As soon as Isaiah got a dollar, he spent it. Or gave it away.

"You'll use the money to buy the products and services created by your classmates."

Isaiah's face fell.

"What kinds of things can we make?" Amy's other best friend, Kelsey Newell, asked.

Ms. Ives liked that question. "The sky's the limit! While you were working on your math challenge just now, I peeked at some of the letters your parents wrote about you. There is a lot of talent in this class. We have artists, writers"—was she looking at Amy?—"and even some budding engineers."

Todd squirmed under her beaming, expectant smile, turned in his direction. Usually he was full of ideas for anything to make or build, but not this time. For some reason, he couldn't think of anything.

"Now, remember, the product you manufacture and sell has to be your *own* idea, not an idea that comes from your parents. This is *your* project, not your mom's or dad's."

Well, that was one thing she didn't have to worry about in Todd's case. It had been six months now since his dad had been laid off from his job as an engineer. From what Todd could see, his dad had pretty much forgotten how to work at anything. At first his time off had seemed like a long vacation, and he was getting severance pay, extra pay the company gave him because he had been laid off, not fired. But because he had worked at that company for only two years, the severance wasn't very much. Now, as the weeks went by with no interviews for Todd's dad, and no income except his unemployment insurance, Todd's mom had gotten a full-time job at the crafts store in the mall. So she wasn't going to be helping with school projects, either.

Isaiah waved his hand again. This time he waved it so hard his chair began to wobble. "I have a great idea! A really great idea. You're not going to believe how great this idea is. Do you want to hear it?"

"No," Ms. Ives said. "I don't want to hear anybody's ideas right now. Just keep developing your ideas. Talk over your ideas with your partners, if you're going to be working with partners."

Isaiah flung his hand into the air again. "But—"

The chair tipped over, with Isaiah in it. He went sprawling onto the floor.

Todd waited to make sure that Isaiah was okay. When Isaiah gave a shaky smile, Todd burst out laughing. He couldn't help it. Isaiah looked so funny, lying there on the floor, like a large upended centipede, or turtle. *Hey, what happened?* the look on his face said. *One minute I'm right side up, and the next . . .*

"Isaiah! That's your third warning!" Ms. Ives was angry now.

"You said you don't give third warnings," Damon Brewer called out. Damon was the kind of kid who loved to correct other people's mistakes.

Ms. Ives looked uncertain. Todd could tell she didn't want to send Isaiah to the office, but also didn't want to violate her own rules.

"Isaiah," she said sorrowfully, "I'm afraid I'll have to send you to the office?"

"That's okay," Isaiah said cheerfully, as if to reassure her that he didn't mind the punishment. This wasn't the first time in his life that Isaiah had been sent to the office. It was never for something he meant to do. It was always for too many accidents, all on the same day—or, this time, all in the same half hour. It seemed so unfair to Todd. Isaiah might be clumsy, but nobody had a better sense of humor or a bigger heart.

Isaiah leaped up from the floor, grabbed the note Ms. Ives handed him, and bounded toward the door.

Unfortunately, as he went he knocked his shoulder into

the row of cardboard Mini-Society buildings, propped up against the wall by his desk. The entire row of buildings, each connected to all the others, fell forward together in one dramatic, catastrophic motion. Squeals and shrieks came from the kids in the nearby desks, trapped underneath.

"Oops," said Isaiah. He turned to try to raise the fallen buildings.

"Go!" Ms. Ives almost shouted. No question mark this time.

A lot of kids were laughing now, but not Todd. He hated it when Isaiah got into trouble. And the collapse of the entire cardboard Mini-Society seemed so much like the collapse, at home, of Todd's entire life.

As she unclipped her house key from the cluster of miniature stuffed animals hanging from the zipper pull of her backpack, Amy felt suddenly shy. In the days when her father had been working and her mother had been a stay-at-home mom, she had known exactly what she would find when she and Todd got home from school. For one thing, the front door wouldn't be locked. Her mother would be there waiting for them, full of questions about their day, and a healthy but delicious snack would be laid out for them on the kitchen table. But now Amy couldn't open the door, and her mother was off at work, and her father might still be in his pajamas, staring at the TV.

"I can't get my dumb key to work," Amy complained to Todd, who stood patiently behind her. They had rung the doorbell, but no one had answered. "I think it's bent, or something."

Todd gave Amy's key a try, and the door opened easily. "Or something," he said with a grin.

Oh, well. There was a reason their mother called Amy her poet and Todd her engineer. Amy could write a poem about keys. Todd could open doors with them. Amy returned Todd's grin.

Wiggy came to greet them. At least Wiggy never changed. Though even as Amy had that thought, she noticed how much more stiffly Wiggy padded up to them these days, and how much longer it took for her to hear them at the door. It made Amy's heart hurt.

"Wiggles!" Amy dropped to the floor and flung her arms around Wiggy's neck. Todd bent down and patted her, too.

Their father appeared in the front hall. "Hey, kids. How was school?" Amy was relieved to see that he was wearing jeans and a T-shirt. His hair, still wet from the shower, was neatly combed, and he had shaved.

"It was okay," Todd said.

Amy gave Wiggy another hug. "It was *not* okay. Tell him about Isaiah."

"What happened to Isaiah?" their father asked.

When Todd didn't answer, Amy said, "We have this whole row of cardboard buildings in our room for Mini-Society—"

"And Isaiah knocked them over," their father said, with one of his rare smiles.

"How did you know?"

"I took a wild guess."

"It was about the tenth thing he had knocked over in five minutes," Amy said. "Ms. Ives sent him to the office to see the principal."

"What did the principal do?"

"I don't know." Amy looked at Todd. "What *did* Ms. Henderson do?"

Todd shrugged. "Nothing. She knows Isaiah. He can't change how he is."

"I don't know about that," their father said. "People change all the time."

Amy saw Todd open his mouth and close it again. She knew he wanted to say: *You sure changed. And we wish you'd change back again, to the way you were before.* Amy was glad Todd hadn't said anything. When her mother criticized Amy's father, it only made everything worse.

"Do you want a snack?" their father asked awkwardly.

"What is there?" Amy asked.

Now it was his turn to shrug. "Whatever you can find."

In the kitchen, Amy poured herself a bowl of Cheerios, and Todd poured himself a bowl of Grape-Nuts and went to the fridge to get the milk. "The milk's all gone," he reported coldly. "Didn't you go to the store?"

"I guess I didn't get around to it," their father said, a pained, shamed flush rising in his face. Amy saw the grocery list still hanging on the fridge.

Todd set the empty milk jug on the counter and, without another word, left the room. Amy watched him go, half wanting to follow him, to comfort him, half wanting to stay behind, to comfort their dad.

"I didn't realize we were so low on milk," their father said.

"That's okay," Amy told him, trying to sound confident and cheerful. To make it seem okay, she swallowed a big mouthful of dry, hard Cheerios. But then she left the rest of her cereal on the counter next to Todd's untouched bowl of Grape-Nuts and slipped away upstairs.

. . .

When Amy arrived at school the next morning, Kelsey and Julia were waiting for her. One quick giggle of greeting for Todd—Amy knew they both thought he was cute—and they dragged her off to their favorite meeting spot behind the spruce tree, at the edge of the school property.

"We have the best idea for Mini-Society!" Kelsey announced. She was the shortest of the three, with brown pigtails that stuck straight out on either side of her head. Kelsey could be an elf in one of Amy's stories.

"What is it?"

"Wait till you hear it," Julia said. Tall and blond and beautiful, Julia could be a princess in one of Amy's stories. "We're going to sell thousands!" she said.

"Millions!" Kelsey corrected.

Amy waited for them to tell her what it was. She tried to swallow the thought that if the three of them were going to be partners, they should have come up with the idea for their product together. If she had thought of something herself, she would have gone running to them with *her* idea.

"Frizzy Fred," Julia said, emphasizing each syllable.

"Frizzy Fred," Amy repeated blankly.

"Show her," Kelsey said.

From her backpack Julia produced a pencil, with some kind of frizzy, fuzzy hot-pink hair glued over its—his?—eraser. No face, just hair.

"This is Fred," Julia said. "Fred, this is Amy."

"Show her what he does," Kelsey urged.

Between her hands, Julia rolled the pencil—Fred's thin, yellow body—back and forth, back and forth, until his hair billowed out around his "head" in a great frizzy cloud of blinding pink. Amy thought it was mildly funny: this skinny yellow pencil with his big pink hurricane of hair. Both Kelsey and Julia shrieked with laughter.

"We're going to sell billions," Julia said, once Fred had calmed down and every hair had been smoothed back into place.

"Trillions!" Kelsey said. "So what do you think?"

"I think it's . . . great." Maybe she'd like the idea better if the others hadn't thought it up without her. Maybe she could make herself like it better if she wrote a story about Fred: *Once upon a time there was a pencil named Frizzy Fred.* No. Amy didn't want to write a story about a pencil named Fred with fake pink hair glued onto his eraser.

The bell rang, and they ran to the fifth-grade door.

"What's Todd going to make?" Kelsey asked Amy.

"I don't know. Something complicated, probably. With gears. Or pulleys. Or batteries."

"What do you think Violet will make?" Kelsey asked.

"I know!" Julia could hardly say it for laughing. "A decorated Kleenex box!"

Amy laughed, too. Violet was always crying about something: about every word she got wrong on a spelling test, every math problem she didn't understand. She had even cried when she'd gotten an odd-shaped piece of French toast in the school cafeteria.

With a big smile, Ms. Ives opened the door to her class. "Come in, everybody! Welcome back to another great day of Mini-Society!"

Amy hoped, for both the teacher's and Isaiah's sake, that the Mini-Society buildings would stay erect today.

"Don't tell anyone about Frizzy Fred," Kelsey whispered to Amy as they headed into their classroom.

"I won't," Amy whispered back.

. . .

On that day they weren't going to have Mini-Society time until after lunch. Amy ate lunch with Kelsey and Julia. Unfortunately, Violet sat down at their table, too. Maybe she was tired of sitting alone. Amy couldn't really blame her.

"Hi, Violet!" Amy forced a friendly smile. "How's it going?"

"Not so good."

Why couldn't Violet say "Okay" like an ordinary person? If someone said "Okay," you could move on to another subject, like what you were reading, or what you were going to wear tomorrow. If someone said "Not so good," you had to ask "What's wrong?"

"What's wrong?"

Kelsey and Julia started talking to each other across the table, as if Amy and Violet weren't there. Amy didn't blame them. Why should all three of them have to listen to Violet?

"The math problem your brother got right this morning? I didn't understand a single thing he was talking about." Sure enough, Violet's voice sounded choked with tears.

Well, that was nothing to cry about. If Amy cried every

time Todd solved a math problem she couldn't, she'd be crying all the time.

"Neither did I. But that's just Todd. He's really good in math. He's going to be an engineer someday."

"I couldn't think of anything to write for that story about the big box."

Now, *that* was a problem Amy couldn't understand. Ms. Ives had told them to finish a story that began, "One day a huge box arrived in the mail addressed to me, and when I finally got the box opened, I saw that it was . . ." Amy's pencil had flown across the page. Although the box was huge, the important thing it contained, wrapped in layer after layer of cotton batting, was a magic ring, which could grant three wishes . . .

"My story went: I saw that it was the winter coat my mother had ordered from a catalog. The end."

Amy laughed. Then she realized that Violet hadn't meant to be funny.

"I can't think of a Mini-Society product, either."

"We just came up with our idea this morning." Well, Amy had just heard about it that morning. Kelsey and Julia had obviously come up with it last night. And Amy still wasn't sure that she liked Frizzy Fred all that much.

"I wish I had someone to work with. But nobody ever picks me to be their partner for anything."

Was Violet hinting that Amy ask her to join their group? She couldn't. Julia and Kelsey would never want to be in a group with Violet. Who would?

"Todd never works with a partner," Amy said, "even

though he's best friends with Isaiah. He likes to work by himself on school projects, and he always comes up with something amazing."

Violet gave a loud, wet, teary sniff. "I'm not going to come up with anything amazing."

Amy had to admit that Violet was probably right.

Julia and Kelsey were standing up to carry their trays to the conveyer belt and head outside for lunch recess. "Bye, Violet," Amy said hastily.

"Bye, Amy," Violet said, blinking back tears.

. . .

After lunch Ms. Ives had the class get out their Mini-Society folders. Amy found hers right away, and Isaiah managed to get his out without knocking over any furniture, though Ms. Ives kept shooting nervous looks in his direction.

"I know you're all starting to come up with some wonderful ideas for your products," Ms. Ives said. "Remember, you can have a business alone, as a *sole proprietor*, or be in a *partnership* with one other person."

*One* other person? Amy's hand shot up at the same time that Kelsey and Julia began waving theirs.

"Yes, girls?"

"Can you work with *two* other people?" Kelsey asked. "Amy and Julia and I want to work together."

Ms. Ives looked uncertain for a moment, and then said, "You can work *alone*, or in groups of *two*. I don't want the groups any larger than that."

"But we already have our idea and everything!" Julia burst out.

"I'm sorry, girls." Ms. Ives sounded more confident than usual. "One of you will have to come up with a different idea. There are thousands of ideas out there, believe me. Now, which one of you is willing to be in a different group?"

There was a long, strained pause. Then, "I'll be in a different group," Amy said slowly. Frizzy Fred belonged to Kelsey and Julia. They were the ones who had thought him up, wild pink hair and all.

Kelsey and Julia looked relieved. Amy felt even worse.

"Great! Who wants to be partners with Amy?"

*Wait!* Amy wanted to say. Things were happening too fast. She could find her own partner. She never had any trouble finding partners. She could work with Todd if she had to. Pulleys and gears wouldn't be worse than Frizzy Fred would have been. For that matter, she could work alone. Lots of kids were probably working alone. Suddenly Amy had a great idea for a sole-proprietor business: she could write and sell special-order stories about all the other kids in the class.

It was too late.

Violet LaFarge put up her hand.

Ms. Ives smiled brightly. "I knew everything would work out. Thank you, Violet!"

Amy stared at her lap, willing herself not to cry. One crybaby in their partnership was more than enough. She wouldn't let herself look at Julia or Kelsey, though she could feel their pity radiating toward her.

*Now* was the time for the Mini-Society buildings to come tumbling down.

But they kept right on standing.

On Friday after school, Todd had soccer practice, to get ready for the first game of the season the next day. The team had played together, with almost all the same guys on it, since kindergarten, and last year they had had an undefeated season. It was wonderful to be outside, running up and down the field, under the clear, cloudless Colorado sky, looking forward to another win.

Damon's dad was the coach. Todd thought he was a pretty good coach, even if sometimes he favored Damon over the other kids. Todd's dad probably would have favored Todd if he had been the coach. But Todd's dad had always been too busy with his job to have time to coach anything. Anyway, Damon was a great player. In Todd's opinion, Damon was the second best player on the team.

After Todd.

It wasn't bragging, Todd figured, to think something that was true.

Isaiah wasn't on the team, luckily for the team, and for Isaiah, even for the ball. Although soccer balls were pretty hard to destroy, Todd had a feeling Isaiah could manage to do it somehow. But Todd wished that Isaiah were on the team, anyway.

Todd's dad picked him up after practice and dropped him off at Isaiah's on the way home. Todd still wasn't used to having his dad drive him places, while his mom was at work.

After Todd and Isaiah defeated level six in Isaiah's newest video game, they lay on the floor in the family room waiting for the pizza guy to show up. Isaiah's family had pizza every Friday night.

"I wish I could make my own video game for my Mini-Society product," Isaiah said. "It could be this sort of attack-of-the-aliens game, only kids from school would be the aliens. Like, Damon would be the Know-It-All Alien. And you'd get points when you zapped him and showed he was wrong about something. And Violet would be the Crying Alien, and you'd get zapped if she cried on you."

"Who would we be?" Todd asked.

"I'd be the Klutz Alien, and people would get zapped if I tripped on them. And you'd be the Boy Genius Alien, who designed the best zapper." Isaiah was starting to sound excited. "Do you think we really could? Make our own video game?"

"No," Todd said. You didn't have to be a Boy Genius to know that two fifth graders couldn't make a real video game, with no help from any grownups.

Isaiah sighed heavily.

"What was the idea you had the other day?" Todd asked. "The one Ms. Ives didn't want to hear?"

"Oh, that one. I decided it was stupid."

"What was it? Maybe it wasn't stupid."

"Well, you know how I have, like, ten thousand broken crayons?"

No, Todd hadn't known that, but he nodded.

"Janie keeps breaking them"—Isaiah had a four-year-old sister—"and I guess over the years I probably broke some, too."

Todd swallowed a smile.

"So I thought I could melt them down and form these crayon lumps. You could use them for paperweights, or weapons, or decorations, and even color with them, too. They'd be a novelty item."

"Crayon lumps."

"I'd give them a different name. Like Crayon Creations. Maybe I could make them in different shapes, pour them into molds or something, if I could find some molds. Like duck-shaped molds. Or chickens! I think a lot of people would like a big crayon chicken. So what do you think? Hey, I don't know why I thought this was stupid. It isn't stupid! It's great!"

Well, crayon chickens were probably better than crayon lumps.

"Where would you get the chicken molds?" Todd asked practically.

"At the crafts store where your mom works. They proba-bly sell all kinds of molds. Chickens. Sheep. Cows. Pigs. I could make a whole crayon farm. Crayon Critters!"

Actually, the idea didn't sound stupid. Todd wondered if

he should worry that for once one of Isaiah's ideas didn't sound stupid. It seemed a bad omen, somehow.

. . .

Todd woke up earlier than usual on Saturday morning, knowing there was something important he had to remember. To let Wiggy out so she wouldn't pee on the living room carpet? The older Wiggy got, the more accidents she had. But he could hear his mother rattling dishes down in the kitchen, so she would have already taken care of Wigs.

The game!

Todd's team wasn't playing until ten, but Todd still sprang out of bed and hurried to the window. The sky in the east was a rosy pink, the kind of sunrise Amy was always writing poems about.

"You're up early," his mother greeted him as he came into the kitchen. Wiggy thumped her tail. Todd felt sorry for people who didn't have a dog's tail go wild with joy at the sight of them.

"Big game today," Todd explained. Every game was a big game when you planned on having another undefeated season.

"Todd, I—" His mother stopped. Todd noticed that her eyes were red, as if she had been peeling onions—or crying? "I can't go. To the game. I tried to switch my hours at the store, but Saturdays— I'm just too new there to take off a Saturday."

"That's okay." His mom had come to all his games over the past five years. It didn't matter if she missed one. At least, it didn't matter to him. It certainly seemed to matter to his mother.

"Do you know that I have never missed a single one of your games? Ever?"

Todd nodded.

"Until today." Her eyes filled with tears. So she *had* been crying! Because she had to miss the game? Todd couldn't believe it. But then Todd himself never cried. It was as if he couldn't. He and Violet LaFarge were opposites that way: the girl who always cried, the boy who never cried.

"Everybody's parents miss a game now and then," Todd told her. His father had missed most of them.

"Not me," his mother said, turning away from him toward the sink.

Suddenly Todd got it. Just the way his team wanted a perfect, undefeated season of playing soccer, his mother wanted a perfect, undefeated season of being a mom. A perfect, undefeated *lifetime* of being a mom.

"It's okay," Todd said. "It's really okay. Dad can come, right?"

"I guess so." Her voice was tight. "It isn't as if he has anything else to do. Though it wouldn't be a bad idea to have someone run a vacuum around here one of these days."

One of these days, maybe, but not on a soccer-game day.

"And Amy's coming," Todd pointed out.

"I think Kelsey and Julia are coming with her," his mother said, turning back toward him and forcing a smile.

"Then just about everyone will be there." Todd tried to

make his tone reassuring, but as soon as the words came out, he realized he had said the wrong thing.

"Yes," his mother said stiffly. "Everyone but me."

. . .

Next time, Todd decided, he wasn't going to ride to a game with Amy and Kelsey and Julia all giggling together in the backseat. It was hard to get his mind focused on soccer when every two seconds all three girls started shrieking with laughter.

"I wrote a song about Frizzy Fred," Julia said.

Shrieks of laughter. Todd didn't know who Frizzy Fred was, but he wasn't about to ask. There was no one in their class at school named Fred. And no boy whose hair was frizzy.

"Sing it," Kelsey urged.

More shrieks.

"I can't!"

"Oh, come on, sing it!"

Shrieks, shrieks, shrieks. Then Julia started singing, in her high-pitched, slightly off-key voice, "I love you, Fre-e-d, oh, yes I do. I don't love anyone like I love you. When you're not near to me, I'm blue. Oh, Frizzy Fred, I love you!"

As the girls exploded into laughter this time, it struck Todd that he didn't hear Amy. He didn't think she had been laughing before, either. He gave a quick glance over his shoulder: Amy was smiling, but even the smile seemed to be an effort. Kelsey and Julia were laughing too hard to notice.

"Okay," his dad said, "you got me. Who, or what, is Frizzy Fred?"

"He's very handsome," Julia said.

"And very talented," Kelsey said.

"And very thin!"

"And you can buy him at our first Mini-Society selling session!"

Okay. So now Todd knew who—what—Frizzy Fred was: some dumb thing to sell at Mini-Society. But what he didn't know was why Julia and Kelsey would go on and on about their Mini-Society idea when it was clear to Todd, and should have been clear to them, that it was making Amy feel bad. Todd wasn't going to buy a Frizzy Fred from them, that was for sure, whatever Frizzy Fred turned out to be.

The game was a tough one, against the only team in the league that had almost beaten Todd's team the year before. The score was 2–1 at the half, with Todd's team behind.

He saw his dad standing alone on the sidelines, not talking to any of the other dads. His dad probably didn't know what to talk to them about. His mom was the one who knew all the other parents, and every detail about their children's after-school activities, and which teacher each child had at school this year, and which new fund-raiser the PTO was thinking of trying. Todd doubted that his dad even knew his own kids' teacher's name. Or what the letters PTO stood for.

As Todd chugged down some water, he felt a hand on his shoulder. It was his dad.

"Good job," his dad said awkwardly.

"I missed that one pass." The score might have been tied 2–2 if he had made it.

"I think you did a good job," his dad repeated.

Todd felt a small surge of gratitude toward his dad for saying so little. His mom would have said, "Good job, honey. Too bad about that one pass. You must feel terrible. But Damon should have been watching more closely before he sent the ball your way. It really wasn't your fault. I hope his dad knows it wasn't your fault. Just do your best in the second half. Try to pay a little more attention, that's all . . ."

He remembered last year, when his dad had helped him on his project for the science fair. Todd had built a race car powered by a mousetrap—you'd spring the mousetrap, and the car would speed forward—and his dad had been really great to work with, letting Todd come up with all his own ideas, listening to his ideas without saying too much, asking a few questions but letting Todd find his own answers. It had been a lot of fun, being two engineers together, tinkering with that little mousetrap car and getting it to run as fast and as far as possible. But now his dad wasn't an engineer anymore. Maybe he'd never be an engineer again.

His dad gave Todd's shoulder another pat and went back to the sidelines, his hands thrust deep in his pockets, his shoulders hunched against the unexpectedly chilly wind that had just come up.

Todd's team won the game, 3–2.

**I** have to work the closing shift tonight," Amy's mother announced on Wednesday morning, her marker poised to write instructions on the dry-erase board. "That means the three of you are on your own for dinner."

For the first few weeks of the new job, Amy's mother had left them casseroles to microwave whenever she had to work late, but this time there was no casserole.

"Try to think of something," Amy's mother said to Amy's father. Amy couldn't remember the last time her father had fixed a meal for anybody. He made no reply.

"All right!" Amy's mother said brightly. "Have a great day, everybody."

Amy saw that the classified ads section of the paper was open on the kitchen table, with a few items circled in bright red, by her mother. But now there were dirty dishes from breakfast piled on top of it.

. . .

At school, they had their first math quiz of the new school year. Amy thought she did pretty well. It helped that she wasn't in the top math group, the one with Todd in it.

When it was time for social studies, Ms. Ives said, "Now, by next Friday I'm going to need a brief description of the product or service you're going to be selling in Mini-Society."

*Nothing,* Amy thought, chewing at her pinky fingernail. You couldn't have a description much briefer than that.

"If you're working with a partner, the two of you need to get together as soon as possible to start brainstorming."

Amy felt Violet's big teary eyes boring into the back of her neck. But she couldn't force herself to turn around and give Violet a cheery grin. She didn't want to get together with Violet to start brainstorming. She didn't want to make a product for Mini-Society with Violet. She didn't want to be in the same fifth-grade class as Violet. She didn't want to live on the same planet as Violet.

"So, when do you want to get together?" Violet asked Amy as soon as Ms. Ives had dismissed the class for lunch.

*Never.*

Julia and Kelsey were already at the head of the lunch line.

"Maybe tomorrow? After school?" Amy suggested. She should have said, How about now? and gotten the whole thing over with, but she couldn't bear having Julia and Kelsey see her eating lunch with Violet again.

Violet looked as if Amy had suggested meeting at Cinderella's castle at Disney World. This was probably the closest Violet had ever come to an actual play date. Amy wished she could really like Violet LaFarge and want to be her friend. But she couldn't.

"Your house or mine?" Violet asked carefully, as if she had practiced the line from some book for unpopular girls on how to make social conversation.

Amy wasn't sure how to answer. She could hardly imagine going to Violet's house. What would it be like? She had a fleeting vision of a dark, gloomy, half-ruined mansion, with heavy creaking shutters on each window, blocking out any hint of daylight. But Amy's own house was so strange these days, too, with her mother at work and her father wandering around like an unshaven ghost.

"Either one." Amy shrugged.

"Come to my house, then. My mother keeps asking why I never have a friend over."

Only Violet would come right out and admit that she didn't have any friends. The first thing a book for unpopular girls would tell you is not to admit you're unpopular.

*I'm not exactly your friend,* Amy wanted to say.

"Okay," she said instead.

"This is going to be great!" Violet gushed. "Right, pardner?"

*Pardner?* If you weren't someone's friend, you also weren't their pardner.

"Right," Amy echoed faintly.

. . .

Amy went to Kelsey's house after school with Julia, and Todd had soccer practice. When she got home, at six o'clock, it was obvious that nothing was happening in the kitchen. Their father was lying on the couch in the family room, watching the news on TV. Todd was doing his math homework on the floor.

"What are we going to do about dinner?" Todd asked.

Amy waited to see what their father would say.

"What do you two want to eat?" He didn't look away from the screen.

"We could call out for pizza," Amy offered.

"Too expensive."

"What else is there?" Todd asked.

"I don't know."

At least he clicked off the TV and followed them to the refrigerator. The three of them stood gazing at its half-empty shelves: catsup, mustard, grape jelly, the end of a ham that had seen better days, a wilted head of lettuce, four boxes of stick margarine bought on sale, yogurts of a brand that nobody liked.

Silently they shut the refrigerator door and trailed over to the pantry cupboard: three cartons of cereal, each of them empty except for the fine, powdery crumbs at the bottom of the box that nobody wanted to eat; several cans of cream of mushroom and cream of chicken soup, which their mother used for making casseroles; a few boxes of Jell-O, but Amy knew that Jell-O took hours to set; two bags of spaghetti—no jars of spaghetti sauce; an assortment of specialty vinegars; olive oil; a dozen cans of Wiggy's favorite brand of dog food.

"This is depressing," their father said.

Amy felt a giggle rising up. It was odd, the way depressing things were less depressing when you came right out and said they were depressing.

"Wait!" Todd reached behind the dog food cans and

pulled out a box of microwave popcorn. "Ta-dah! Dinner will be ready in"—he checked the side of the box—"three minutes, madame and monsieur!"

"Saved!" their father said.

"We can melt this to pour over it." Amy grabbed a stick of margarine from the fridge.

The popcorn made a delicious supper. Their father even found a couple of Granny Smith apples in the crisper to go with it. Nothing tasted better than a handful of buttery, salty popcorn, followed by a slice of tart, firm apple, followed by another handful of popcorn.

Amy felt suddenly hopeful, even about Mini-Society. "I wish there were some way to get out of working with Violet," she told the other two as she set her empty popcorn bowl down on the family room carpet. She didn't know whether her mother would have been more shocked and dismayed by *what* they had eaten for dinner or by *where* they had eaten it. "No food in the family room" was one of her most sacred rules. But her dad didn't seem to care about sacred rules anymore.

"There is," Todd said.

"What is it? How do I do it?"

"Easy. You say to Violet, 'I've decided I want to work alone.'"

"'I've decided I want to work alone,'" Amy repeated.

"That's it," Todd said. "Problem solved."

"What do I say for why I've decided to work alone?"

"You don't have to say why. You've decided you want to work alone. Period."

Amy tried it out again. "I've decided I want to work alone. Do I say this before or after I go to her house tomorrow?"

"Before. I mean, isn't that the whole idea? Not to have to go to her house?"

"What's the matter with Violet?" their father asked then. "Why don't you want to work with her?"

"Violet is—" Amy began.

"A crybaby," Todd finished.

"She cries, like—"

"All the time."

"I hate to say this," their father said, "but don't you think she's going to cry when you tell her you don't want to work with her?"

"Yes," Todd said unhesitatingly. "Violet would cry if you said, 'Good morning, how are you?'"

Todd was right, but that didn't make Amy feel any better about the upcoming conversation. Still, better one teary scene with Violet, followed by freedom, than tears, tears, and more tears over the course of the next few weeks.

"I've decided I want to work alone," Amy practiced.

"Perfect," Todd said.

Wiggy padded over and ate the few pieces of popcorn that had spilled on the carpet.

"I've decided I want to work alone."

She *could* say it, she *could*!

Wiggy thumped her tail approvingly. Todd gave Amy a confident thumbs-up. Their father looked uncertain.

. . .

Before school the next day, Amy walked up to Violet on the playground. *I've decided I want to work alone.*

"Wait till you see the snacks my mother is making for us!" Violet said, beaming. "She has this cookbook from some famous restaurant in San Francisco, with all these delicious and elegant snacks in it. They're called hors d'oeuvres. That's French, I think, for fancy snacks. And we're going to use real china and real silverware. And linen napkins that you have to iron."

So much for telling Violet *before* going to her house.

"I don't want her to go to any trouble," Amy said slowly.

"My mother loves going to trouble! She's been waiting for this moment for years!"

Amy took a deep breath. "It's just that I . . ."

"You *are* coming over, aren't you?"

"Well, I . . ." *Just say it!*

Violet's eyes filled. She could have been a crying doll, where you press a hidden button and the tears start trickling down its pink plastic face.

"You have to come! My mother will die if you don't come!"

"I'm coming, but . . ."

"It's okay if you can't stay long. It's okay if you have to leave early."

Amy gave up. "I'm coming."

It took a moment for the tear-stopping button to work. One big fat tear slipped down Violet's cheek and disappeared underneath her collar.

"Great!" Violet said.

Violet's mother turned out to be short and plump, wearing a pink-flowered dress.

"Come in, Amy, come in! We're so glad to have you! It's such a treat to have a visit from one of Violet's friends!"

From Violet's only friend. From Violet's only friend who wasn't a friend, just a Mini-Society partner. And not even a Mini-Society partner after today. But Violet's mother was apparently much better at pretending than Violet was.

Far from being a gloomy, boarded-up mansion perfect for crying in, Violet's house was sunny and bright and painfully neat. Every magazine on the coffee table was lined up in a row. Every African violet on the table by the window was exactly the same height. Violet's desk at school was painfully neat, too, as opposite from Amy's as desks could get.

Violet's mother took Violet's backpack and hung it on a special hook, with a little engraved sign hanging from it, saying *Violet's Backpack* in an elegant script. There were no other signs hanging on any other hooks. Violet was an only child. Then her mother straightened the ribbon on Violet's one thick braid.

"Let me put out your hors d'oeuvres," Violet's mother said, gesturing toward the dining room table. It was a long, shiny table, with two woven place mats set before the chairs at the farthest end, facing each other. On each place mat sat a delicate plate of pink-flowered china and a matching teacup and saucer. The silverware gleamed like real silver. The napkins were folded into stiff little tents.

Shyly Amy slipped into the chair across from Violet. She waited to see if Violet's mother would put Violet's napkin on her lap for her, but Violet did that herself, at least.

Her mother began bringing out tray after tray of snacks: shrimp wrapped in bacon, strawberries dipped in chocolate, radishes carved to look like pale roses.

"Oh, I hope these are good!" she said anxiously. "Violet darling, sit up straighter. You want to have good posture when Amy's here. Amy, what would you like? Some shrimp? One of these strawberries?"

Amy remembered fairy tales where once you ate the first bite of the enchanted food, you had to stay in the witch's castle forever. She knew that if she ate one of the hors d'oeuvres, she was going to end up doing her Mini-Society project with Violet LaFarge.

She reached out and took a chocolate-dipped strawberry and put it on her plate.

"Eat up, Amy! There's plenty more in the kitchen!" Violet's mother urged. There was already enough food on the table to feed the entire fifth grade.

With Violet's damp, hopeful eyes on her, Amy ate her strawberry, and then reached for another.

So did you say it?" Todd asked Amy when she walked into the family room right before dinner. Dinner was going to be pizza delivery, even though their father had said the other day that pizza was too expensive. Their mother wasn't cooking, their father wasn't cooking, and Todd and Amy and Wiggy weren't cooking. Pizza it had to be.

One look at Amy's face told Todd that she hadn't. How hard could it be to say seven little words to someone? Seven little words that would save you weeks of misery. Every year when they had some project at school, Isaiah wanted to work with Todd, and every year Todd told him, "I've decided I want to work alone." Friendship was one thing, self-destruction another. Todd always came up with a terrific project, and Isaiah always came up with a terrible project, and through it all they stayed best friends. If Todd could say no to Isaiah, why couldn't Amy say no to Violet?

"It was impossible." Amy buried her face in Wiggy's fur. Wiggy thumped her tail. Wiggy was an extremely nonjudgmental dog.

"Amy—"

"You couldn't have done it, either," Amy snapped at him.

"They had napkins shaped like tents! Silverware made out of real silver! Strawberries dipped in chocolate!"

"So?"

"You can't wipe your mouth on someone's linen napkin and then refuse to be their Mini-Society partner," Amy explained wearily.

Todd didn't understand, but he could tell there was no point in making Amy feel worse than she did already.

From the kitchen he could hear his mother's raised voice: "And who's going to pay for this pizza, may I ask? I know all this is hard for you, too, but a crafts store salary isn't exactly enough for a family of four to live on."

"I can pay for it," Todd heard his father say.

"On your unemployment insurance?"

His father didn't answer.

"And another thing," his mother went on. "Why did I find popcorn kernels on the family room carpet this morning? I thought we had a rule about no food in the family room."

Todd tried to close his ears, to avoid hearing whatever sad excuse his father would offer.

"What's your product?" he asked Amy.

"It's bad."

"How bad?"

"Well, I suggested writing stories about people in the class and illustrating them, but Violet said she can't write stories and she hates to draw."

"So what *are* you doing?"

"We're going to use pinecones—Violet's yard has a million pinecones. We're going to dip them in glue and then sprinkle glitter on them. And then when we're done, we'll have sticky, glittery pinecones." Amy glared at Todd. "I already said it was bad, so don't you dare laugh."

Todd tried to think of something positive to say. His parents' voices had gotten louder, but at least they had closed the kitchen door, muffling his mother's sarcasm. "They might be good for Christmas ornaments," he said.

"In September?"

"People's parents might like them."

"Ms. Ives said she's going to tell the parents not to buy things just out of pity for us. We're supposed to learn about supply and demand. If you supply a cool product, there will be a lot of demand for it. If you supply a stupid product, there will be no demand for it. Can you think of anything more stupid than sticky, glittery pinecones?"

"They won't be sticky once the glue dries." But Todd knew that when Amy was in a bad mood, she was bound and determined to make everything sound as hopeless as possible.

"Oh, that's a big comfort. That is just a huge comfort, Todd! Julia and Kelsey are going to sell ten thousand Frizzy Freds, and Violet and I won't sell even one sticky, glittery pinecone."

"I'll buy one."

"All right, we'll sell one."

"Isaiah will buy one."

"*Two* pinecones!" Amy shrieked. She looked as if she was about to say something more; then she turned and ran out of the room.

Todd stared at Wiggy. "What did I say wrong?" he asked the dog. "I mean, really. I was just trying to help."

Someone in their family had to help with something. Wiggy thumped her tail sympathetically.

"Seven words," Todd told Wiggy. "That's all she had to say to save herself from sticky, glittery pinecones. Just seven little words."

. . .

"Our Mini-Society needs a flag!" Ms. Ives said the next day.

Todd groaned. Now she was going to tell them each to come up with a design for a flag, and the class would vote on the designs, and either Amy's friend Julia, who was great at art, or perfect-at-everything Damon would win.

Sure enough, Ms. Ives was starting to pass out sheets of white construction paper.

"Each of you will come up with a design for a flag. Be as creative as you can! And then our class will vote on its favorite design."

*And Julia or Damon will win,* Todd added to himself.

"But there's a twist," Ms. Ives said then.

Someone other than Julia or Damon would win?

"You also have to decide how much you're going to charge the rest of us for your flag design, if it's chosen. In Mini-Society we get paid for what we do."

"Will we know the price of each design before we vote?" Julia asked.

She was probably counting her profits, Todd thought,

though he saw that she was looking at Damon as she spoke. Julia knew who her competition was.

Ms. Ives hesitated. Todd could tell that she couldn't remember the exact instructions in the Mini-Society teacher's manual on this point. "We'll vote on that, too? Yes, in Mini-Society, we make *all* our collective decisions the democratic way, by voting."

"I think we should know the price of each design *before* we vote," Julia said.

"Me too," Kelsey chimed in.

They both looked at Amy.

"Me too," Amy said.

Well, that clearly made sense. It would be stupid to pick one design over another without knowing the price. Not that they were using real money, just fake money they had already voted to call "minis." But still. Knowing the price of something before you bought it made sense.

Damon put up his hand. "*I* think," he said in the superior way he had, as if everyone were especially interested in his thoughts, "we should vote for whichever design we think is *best*. This is our *flag* we're talking about. When our country was founded, George Washington didn't pick the *cheapest* flag. He picked the *best* one."

As if Damon had spent years studying the process by which the Stars and Stripes had been selected.

They voted. Damon's side won, proving, in Todd's opinion, that democracy could come up with some pretty unreasonable results.

"Now, just for inspiration," Ms. Ives said, "I have a handout with some flags from around the world. I want you to see how many kinds there are. And soon there will be twenty-five new and different flag designs for us to consider!"

Todd studied the handout. Most of the flags were rectangular in shape, but there were a couple of wild-shaped ones. Most had plain bars of color, either vertical or horizontal: red, white, and blue; red, white, and green. But some had emblems stuck in the middle of them.

He decided on a plain solid rectangle, with one big spot in the middle, like the flag of Japan. If it was good enough for Japan, it was good enough for Mini-Society.

Each color was supposed to stand for something. On the handout flags, white stood for purity, red for courage, green for hope. If there was one thing Todd didn't feel these days, it was hopeful. One country had black for the hardships its people had suffered. Okay. Todd's flag would be black, with a big yellow dot in the middle. Yellow could stand for money, since Mini-Society was mainly about making money. Money solved hardships for a lot of people. If his father still earned any, maybe his parents could order a pizza without fighting about it for half an hour.

"Put the price of your design on the *back*," Ms. Ives reminded the class.

Todd wrote 50 on his. Fifty minis wasn't very much, but a big yellow spot on a black rectangle wasn't worth very much.

Half an hour later, the flag designs were displayed on the ledges of the chalkboards. Amy had come up with a wreath of flowers against a pale blue background: poetic and pretty, just what he would have expected from Amy. Unfortunately, Julia, Kelsey, *and* Violet had all come up with flower designs, too. Julia's looked the best, because she was so good at drawing. Probably none of the flower designs would win.

Todd had to admit that Damon's design looked as if a grownup had made it, with an elaborate coat of arms in the middle of three vertical color bars. Damon had written a whole page explaining the significance of each one.

Isaiah's flag was orange—for happiness, he said—and it had a funny-looking cartoonish chicken in the middle. Todd had forgotten that Isaiah was pretty good at drawing, too.

"What is the significance of the chicken?" Ms. Ives asked Isaiah.

"It's . . . Well, it can lay eggs, so we'll never be hungry. Or we can eat *it* if we *are* hungry. And . . . I just like drawing chickens."

Everyone laughed.

"All right, turn in your ballots," Ms. Ives told the class.

When she counted the ballots, she looked surprised. "It was close," she said. "Damon, your drawing came in second. But our winner, by one vote, is Isaiah's flag. The—um—one with the chicken."

Todd led the class in a cheer. Isaiah looked stunned. Damon glared at him. It must have been too much for Damon to have his perfectly drawn coat of arms beaten out by a cartoon chicken.

"Oh, the price," Ms. Ives said. "We have to see what we're paying from our classroom treasury for our new flag. Damon, what would you have charged us if your design had won?"

Sullenly, Damon turned his flag over. "A thousand minis."

The class gasped. A thousand minis was a lot of money, even fake money. Good thing Damon's design hadn't won.

"Isaiah, what is the price of yours?"

Grinning, Isaiah turned his over. "Ten thousand minis."

Todd saw a big, messy *10,000* scrawled in crayon. The class was in an uproar now.

"But, Isaiah—" Ms. Ives sputtered. "That's an awful lot for one flag?"

"That's ridiculous!" Damon burst out. "We have to pay *nine* thousand more minis for a flag that got *one* more vote. I think we should vote again, now that we know the prices."

Todd was too mad to raise his hand. "No! It was *your* idea to vote for the flags without knowing the prices. It was a bad idea, but that's what we voted to do. Isaiah's design wins."

Ms. Ives looked from Todd to Damon and back to Todd again. Then she smiled. "I think we're learning some very interesting things from Mini-Society," she said. "Our new flag will be Isaiah's chicken. We'll fly it over our Mini-Society buildings. Isaiah, come to our bank, and Spencer"— the boy who had been voted banker—"will pay you ten thousand minis."

Without knocking over his chair, Isaiah presented himself at the bank.

Todd grinned. They hadn't even had their first selling session yet, and Isaiah—Isaiah!—was already the richest man in town.

When Amy got home after school on Monday afternoon, her mother was there. Because she worked so many Saturdays and Sundays, she usually had a day off during the week. She must have gone grocery shopping, because the house smelled wonderful—like hot, bubbly apples and cinnamon and brown sugar baked together.

"Apple pie?" Amy asked her mother.

"Apple crisp. The first cool day of the fall always makes me want to bake a pan of apple crisp. It's ready now, if you want some. Todd can have his when he gets home from Isaiah's."

Wiggy padded over to greet Amy, as Amy shrugged off her backpack and headed to the kitchen. Maybe she *should* bring Violet over someday, just so Wiggy could make a big, wet, slobbery, tail-thumping fuss over her. Violet wouldn't cry so much if she had a dog like Wiggy to love her. Amy couldn't imagine a dog, or cat, or bird, or guinea pig in Violet's bare and gleaming house, where Violet's mother hovered over her every single minute as if she were a breakable doll—or one of those dolls that cries real tears.

"How was school?" Amy's mother asked.

"Good. Ms. Ives read one of my poems to the class."

"Which one?"

"A new one. It's called 'Autumn Afternoon.' It starts out, 'The sky is gray like billowing smoke. The leaves glow red and gold like flames.' Todd said he didn't understand some of it, but Ms. Ives said it had beautiful imagery."

Amy didn't tell her mother that Ms. Ives had said she was going to submit one of Amy's poems to a contest. She wanted to savor it by herself for a while.

"That Todd," her mother said fondly. "He's an engineer, through and through. But I'm glad I got one poet."

The house felt too quiet. "Where's Dad?"

"He has a job interview." Amy could tell that her mother was trying to keep her tone even, casual, unexcited. "It doesn't sound like the perfect job—he'd be doing even more traveling than he used to—but . . ." Her mother's voice trailed off.

"But if he got it, you could quit your job," Amy finished for her.

"It's not that. It would just be so wonderful for him. My job isn't that bad, really."

"It isn't?" This was the first time Amy had heard her mother say anything good about her job. She still remembered the tears in her mother's eyes when the rest of them had headed out to Todd's first game together, and she had had to miss it because of work.

"I had an interesting conversation with Max yesterday. He's thinking of offering some crafts classes, to bring more people into the store on Saturday mornings, and he asked me if I'd like to teach one of them."

Amy tried to imagine her mother as a teacher. She was certainly a wonderful quilter, and knitter, and there wasn't anything she couldn't do with a glue gun. "What did you say?"

"Well, it might be fun. You know, I majored in home ec. Home economics. I had planned to teach high school— sewing, cooking, all of it. But I married your father right after graduation, and then you and Todd came along, and I loved being home with you so much that I never got around to teaching. And now—well, maybe I'll do some teaching, after all."

"So if Daddy got a job, you *wouldn't* quit yours?"

"I didn't say that. I just said it might be fun to teach a crafts class now and then, that's all."

Amy heard her father's car, purring into the garage. She and her mother both froze. *Please oh please oh please let the interview have gone well.* She heard the car door slam. An angry slam? A joyful slam? You had to slam the Bug's door pretty hard or it didn't shut all the way.

Her father's footsteps, in the hall, sounded slow and discouraged, but they always sounded that way now. Probably they'd sound the same no matter how the interview had gone.

Then Amy saw her father's face. One Christmas, years ago, Todd had wanted a construction toy, and he had torn the wrapping off the biggest box under the tree, and it had turned out to be a dumb toy fire engine from Aunt Anne. His face then had looked the way her father's face looked now.

"So?" her mother asked, and Amy could hear the bitter disappointment in the apparently neutral syllable.

"It was a sales job, dressed up as an engineering job. I'm an engineer, not a salesman. I've never sold anything to anybody in my life."

"What do you think I do all day long at my job?" Amy's mother asked in a dangerously quiet voice. "The Crafts Cottage is a *store*. We *sell* things. *I* sell things. What's wrong with being in sales?"

"Nothing's wrong with being in sales. But *I'm* not a salesman, I'm an engineer."

"An unemployed engineer. An unemployed engineer who till today hadn't had a job interview in two months."

Amy couldn't bear it anymore. She whispered to Wiggy, and even though Wiggy was half-deaf now, the old dog turned and followed Amy out of the room.

"Isn't a sales job better than nothing?" Amy could hear her mother's voice, growing higher with anger.

"Not this one," her father replied, his voice painfully penetrating despite its defeated tone.

Amy went into her room and shut the door behind her. It slammed, but she knew her parents were too busy fighting to analyze the quality of the slam. She didn't know why they had to fight. It was bad enough that the interview had come to nothing. Fighting about it only made it worse.

"Here, Wiggy." Amy patted the place beside her on the bed.

Wiggy tried to jump up, but couldn't make it. Amy got

off the bed and gave her a boost. And then she cried into Wiggy's thick, soft fur.

. . .

"Tell us what your project is," Julia coaxed Amy as Julia, Kelsey, and Amy were walking home together the next day after school. Amy had invited them over to her house, for a change. She could serve them leftover apple crisp. It felt so good to be part of the old threesome.

"It's a secret," Amy said lamely.

"Best friends don't have secrets from each other," Kelsey said.

Amy looked away. *Was* she still best friends with Julia and Kelsey, or were they just best friends with each other?

"It's dumb, anyway," she finally said.

"How dumb is it? Did Violet think of it?" Julia asked.

Kelsey didn't give Amy time to answer. "Did you really go to Violet's house? What was it like? Was everything there, like, all tearstained from Violet crying on it?"

"It was just a house."

"If you don't tell us what your project is, we won't tell you anything else about Frizzy Fred," Julia threatened.

If Amy never heard another word about Frizzy Fred, it would be fine with her.

"I told Violet I wouldn't tell." That wasn't true; she hadn't told Violet anything of the sort. But she felt a sudden, odd burst of loyalty toward her weepy partner. It was bad enough just being Violet LaFarge without having popular girls like Julia and Kelsey laughing at you all day long.

"You told *Violet*?" Julia sounded angry now. "Who are you best friends with, Violet or us?"

*Neither,* Amy wanted to say.

"I'm not friends with Violet. It's just that—if you had a project as dumb as mine, you wouldn't want to tell anyone, either."

Julia and Kelsey exchanged superior glances.

"We understand," Julia said.

"We really do," Kelsey said.

Amy had a moment's misgiving as she fumbled for her key. She hadn't told her father that she was bringing Julia and Kelsey home with her. But she and Todd had never had to ask permission to have friends stop by to visit. Their friends were always welcome.

She managed to get the door open. "Hello?" she called out tentatively. "I'm home!"

There was no answer. Maybe her father had gone out on errands. Maybe he even had another job interview, but hadn't wanted to say anything about it so as not to get their hopes up.

"Do you want some apple crisp?" Amy asked Julia and Kelsey eagerly. She'd heat it up in the microwave, then put vanilla ice cream on it.

"Sure." Julia gave a shrug.

"Maybe a little bit," Kelsey said. "I'm not that big on apples."

Amy's mother had vacuumed yesterday, on her day off, but the kitchen was a disaster area. The breakfast dishes were still sitting on the counter, and her father's lunch dishes, too, and an open can of Wiggy's dog food, and a heap of newspapers her father must have been reading. Amy didn't know if it was better to whisk the dishes into the dishwasher and the papers into the recycling bin, or to carry on as if the mess were invisible. Lots of people had messy kitchens—but not Julia, or Kelsey, or Amy herself, back before her mother had started working.

Amy decided to pretend the mess was invisible. The sooner she could serve her friends some tempting, warm apple crisp, the better. She scooped the apple crisp into three bowls—"Not too much for me, remember," Kelsey said—and popped the first one into the microwave.

"Do you want ice cream with it?" Amy asked.

Julia and Kelsey nodded, but when Amy checked the freezer, there wasn't any ice cream. Her father must have forgotten to add ice cream to the grocery list when he finished the carton, so her mother hadn't bought any yesterday.

"I guess we don't have any ice cream," Amy said.

Julia gave another shrug.

"It's not like I really like apple crisp, anyway," Kelsey said.

Finally, all three bowls of apple crisp—a big one for Amy, a medium one for Julia, and a small one for Kelsey—were heated. Amy glanced at the cluttered kitchen table and said, "Let's go sit in the family room."

"I thought your mother didn't let you eat in the family room," Julia said.

That was the trouble when your friends knew your house rules almost as well as you did.

"Well, she's not here now," Amy said. "I don't think my father's here now, either."

Amy settled herself in the rocking chair, letting her friends have the couch, and took her first big bite. The apple crisp wasn't as good as it had been the day before. The topping had sort of stuck together in a gummy mass over the limp, soggy apples.

"So!" Amy said. "How *are* things coming with good old Fred?"

There was a strange, strangled look on Julia's and Kelsey's faces. Were they really not going to tell her anything more about Fred if she didn't tell them about the sticky, glittery pinecones? But then Amy turned to see what they were looking at.

Her father was standing in the family room doorway. He was wearing his faded pajamas and ratty old bathrobe. He hadn't shaved. His hair, grayer than Amy had ever seen it before, was standing up every which way.

"Hi, Mr. Davidson," Julia said awkwardly.

Kelsey looked too horrified to say anything.

"I'm sorry," Amy's dad said without meeting Amy's eyes. "I didn't realize you had company. You girls were so quiet, I didn't hear any voices . . ." His own voice trailed off.

Amy waited. There was another long, uncomfortable moment, and then her father turned and shuffled back upstairs in his old, favorite, broken-backed slippers.

The girls ate their apple crisp in silence. When they had finished, Amy noticed that there was still plenty left in Julia's bowl, and even in Kelsey's, although she'd only had a few spoonfuls to begin with.

"I guess we'd better go," Julia said.

"We have all that math homework," Kelsey said.

Amy didn't try to talk them into staying. She wanted them gone more than anything in the world.

If only her father would leave, too. No, that wasn't right. If only her real, true father would come back again.

Todd didn't have a single idea for his Mini-Society project. Not one. He knew Amy was expecting him to make some dazzling, clever, mechanical contraption, but whatever he came up with would also have to be something he could manufacture cheaply, and in bulk, *and* that would sell. Something like Crayon Critters.

All he had to do was ask Isaiah, and he could be his friend's partner in Crayon Critters. But that didn't seem fair. Whenever he'd had a better idea than Isaiah, he had told Isaiah he wanted to work alone. Now that Isaiah finally had a better idea than he did, he wanted to work together? No. Isaiah deserved any success he had with Crayon Critters, and he deserved to get full credit for it, too.

"Make little model rockets," Amy suggested Wednesday night after dinner. Their mother had made the dinner—spaghetti with meatballs—so it had been good. Todd had offered Wiggy the lone leftover meatball, but for once Wiggy hadn't seemed hungry. Todd hoped Wiggy wasn't coming down with something.

"Just how would I do that?" It was a mean question, given that Amy was only trying to help.

"How should I know? You're the engineer, not me. It

doesn't have to be a great rocket, just something that goes up in the air and then comes back down again."

"*Everything* that goes up in the air comes back down again. It's called gravity. Sir Isaac Newton discovered it three hundred years ago."

"Okay, then. That makes it even easier. You design the part that makes it go up in the air, and Sir Isaac Newton can make it come down again."

Todd didn't bother commenting on that one. If his dad had been in the room, they would have rolled their eyes at each other. It used to be comforting for Todd and his dad to be the family's two misunderstood scientists—back when his dad had been a scientist.

"Well, you have to think of something. The first selling session is in less than two weeks."

"What if I don't?"

"Don't what?"

"Don't think of anything."

"Then you'll fail!" Amy's voice quavered.

"What's so bad about failing?" Todd asked bitterly. "People fail all the time. Just look at Dad."

This time, Amy didn't say a word.

. . .

Damon had a very Damon-like project. He told Todd and Isaiah all about it during lunch the next day. Damon sat with Todd and Isaiah at lunch sometimes. He tended to rotate, sitting with everybody. Either Damon was the most popular kid in the class, and everybody liked him, or Damon was the least popular kid in the class—except for

Violet—and nobody liked him. Damon evidently saw it the first way.

Todd wouldn't have asked Damon about his product, but Isaiah did.

"Now, don't tell anybody else, okay?" Damon said in a low voice. Todd thought that Damon had probably told everybody else in the class, swearing them all to secrecy.

Isaiah nodded agreeably.

"I got a digital camera last Christmas, and I'm taking pictures of Riverside Elementary from all different angles, and scanning them into the computer, and making wall calendars."

"Wow," Isaiah said.

"Do you think most kids want to buy wall calendars?" Todd couldn't resist asking.

"I think most *parents* want to buy wall calendars. My market surveys say it's the parent market I need to be targeting."

Damon had done market surveys?

"Which is good," Damon went on, "since parents are the ones with the deep pockets."

Isaiah looked at him blankly.

"With the *money*."

This time Isaiah grinned.

"What about you two?" Damon asked.

Isaiah explained about Crayon Critters.

Damon shrugged. "Girls might like them," he conceded. "You could focus on the cute angle. Girls are suckers for anything cute. What about you, Todd?"

Todd couldn't tell Damon what he had told Amy, that he was seriously considering not coming up with any product at all. "I'm still working on it."

Damon gave a low whistle. "You're cutting it pretty close, if you ask me."

Todd *hadn't* asked him.

"I'd get started soon if I were you. Like, yesterday."

"Thanks for the advice," Todd said.

"Do you know how many new businesses in America fail?" Damon asked as he stood up with his tray.

Isaiah shook his head obligingly.

"Ninety percent. Nine out of ten. Catch you later, guys."

Todd was relieved when Damon strolled away.

. . .

Todd was lying on the family room floor doing math homework, when he heard his mother, back from her shift at the Crafts Cottage. She was later than usual, so she must have stopped on the way home to get groceries. Todd hoped so. Groceries were one of life's good things.

Math homework was another. Todd knew other kids thought it was strange to like having math homework, but he did. He loved questions that had answers, problems that had solutions, twenty of them, all on one page. He loved looking at a neat page of calculations and knowing that he had them all one hundred percent right.

His mother came into the family room and clicked off the TV. Todd looked at Amy, so lost in her book that she didn't seem to register their mother's presence in the room.

But their father, dozing on the couch with the remote in his hand, came awake with a guilty startle.

"David. Todd. Amy." Quiet voices could sound so much more menacing than shouting ones. "I need you to come into the kitchen. Now."

Amy put her book down then, and the three of them straggled into the kitchen. If they had had tails like Wiggy, the tails would have been tucked between their legs.

"Look at this place," Todd's mother said.

It was bad: newspapers in an untidy heap on the table, dirty dishes everywhere, an empty milk carton standing on the counter next to spilled cereal left over from breakfast, and two sacks of groceries his mom had just carried in from the car.

"I want this cleaned up. I want these groceries put away. I want a decent meal with every part of the food pyramid represented on the table in sixty minutes. Call me when it's ready. I'm going to be upstairs soaking in a hot tub."

Then she was gone.

Once his first spasm of remorse had passed, Todd actually felt relieved. It was so much better to be doing something rather than nothing, to be solving a problem rather than pretending it didn't exist. He opened the dishwasher and started loading dirty dishes into it, as Amy and their father took the groceries out of the paper sacks and put them on the pantry shelves and in the fridge.

"How does the food pyramid work?" their father broke the silence to ask.

"You're supposed to eat a lot of grains and cereals," Todd

explained. They had studied the food pyramid at school last year. "They're on the bottom of the pyramid, the wide part. And hardly any fats and sugars. They're the little point at the top. And eat lots of vegetables and fruits. And some protein, too."

"I don't think she really cares if we have the whole pyramid," Amy said. "Just so it looks sort of balanced. I mean, not just popcorn and apples."

"Maybe we should look in a cookbook," their father suggested.

There was a whole bookcase full of cookbooks against one kitchen wall. It was hard to know where to begin. Some of them were as thick as dictionaries; others had obviously unhelpful titles such as *Fifty Christmas Cookies from One Basic Dough* or *Easy Entertaining*.

"Here's one," Todd said. He pulled out *Thirty-Minute Meals*.

Their father glanced at the clock on the microwave. "Can you find one that says *Fifteen-Minute Meals*?"

Todd checked the shelves again. "Nope. The only other one that tells the minutes is the *Sixty-Minute Gourmet*."

"Okay, thirty minutes it is."

"Let's make something with chicken," Amy said. "I just put away a lot of chicken."

"How about curried chicken breasts with rice?" Todd asked. It looked good in the picture. "Do we have any rice?"

"Right here!" their father answered.

"What about fruits and vegetables?" Amy reminded them.

"We'll have broccoli on the side," their father said.

"Dairy products?" Todd thought the pyramid had dairy products on it somewhere.

"You kids can drink milk. And look, there's some cream in the sauce. Do we have any cream?"

Amy checked the fridge. "We have half-and-half. That's sort of like cream."

The meal took more than thirty minutes to make. It turned out that the thirty minutes started *after* you had chosen the recipe, located the ingredients, and done whatever preliminary chopping you had to do, which for curried chicken breasts was a lot. Still, forty-five minutes later, their father sent Amy upstairs to summon their mother for dinner.

When she came into the kitchen, she stared in apparent disbelief. "You even fixed broccoli," she whispered.

"We cooked it too long," Todd's father confessed. "But it still counts as a vegetable."

When they started eating, Todd noticed that if the broccoli had been cooked too long, the rice hadn't been cooked long enough: it was hard and grainy. And the chicken breasts were a little tough. He didn't know if that meant they had been cooked too long, or not long enough.

"This is delicious!" his mother exclaimed after the first bite.

That was definitely an exaggeration.

"Um . . . how exactly are you defining *delicious*?" his father asked.

"My definition of *delicious* is food cooked by someone else."

At least it was edible, which Todd knew was more than his mother had allowed herself to expect. There weren't even any leftovers for Wiggy. Overcooked, limp broccoli and undercooked, grainy rice drowned in curry sauce probably wasn't her favorite dish, anyway. But right then, with his whole family sitting around the table together in the lamplight, and Wiggy lying on the floor beside him, it tasted pretty good to Todd.

. . .

"Todd." Ms. Ives stopped by his desk on Friday. "You didn't turn in the description of your product. I'm going to have to take off points for every day it's late. Our first selling session is a week from Monday, you know."

"I know."

"Is something wrong?"

Todd shook his head.

"Your parents have told me what a talented young engineer you are! I can't wait to hear what great idea you've come up with!"

Why was it that the more people talked about Todd's great ideas, the fewer great ideas he actually had? The higher people's expectations, the harder it was to live up to them.

Ms. Ives beamed encouragingly at him. This must be the moment when he was supposed to reveal his brilliant plan.

When Todd didn't respond, a hint of worry crept into Ms. Ives's eyes. "Todd, you do have an idea for your product, don't you?"

"Well . . . not exactly."

"But there are so many wonderful products you could

sell! Hundreds of them! Why don't you make—" She stopped, apparently remembering that students were required to come up with their own products and not use ideas generated by parents or teachers. "I just know you can come up with something splendid!"

"I'll try," Todd said, hoping she'd be satisfied and move on.

"That's the right attitude!" But the enthusiasm in her voice didn't match the lingering concern in her face. At least she did leave him alone then and bustle off to check on someone else.

He had said he'd try. But if Damon was right, nine out of ten businesses ended in failure. In Todd's opinion, that didn't make a person feel like racing out into the world and trying. It made a person feel like giving up before he even started—especially when his own dad had already given up, when his own dad, his fellow scientist, his fellow engineer, had given up on work completely.

On the playground before school on Monday, Amy was heading toward Julia and Kelsey when Violet intercepted her.

"We need to start work on our pinecones!" Violet announced. "My mother and I went out yesterday after church and collected some."

"How many?" Amy asked, just to say something.

"About three hundred."

"Three *hundred*?" One for Todd, one for Isaiah, and 298 left over?

"Well, it's better to have too many than not enough. We don't have to put glitter on all of them right away. We can wait and see how it goes."

Amy decided not to offer any predictions. "We need to get the glue and the glitter." One *tiny* bottle of each.

"Do you want to go shopping for them together? Like, today after school? We can go to the Crafts Cottage."

"My mother works at the Crafts Cottage. She can bring stuff home if we tell her what we want."

"Your mother works at the Crafts Cottage?" Violet seemed overcome with awe. "That's my favorite store. I love the Crafts Cottage! Do you know what my favorite thing in the whole world is?"

Amy shook her head.

"Just guess!"

Amy didn't want to guess.

"Felt! I love felt! All those bright-colored squares of felt, only twelve cents each."

Well, Amy did like felt herself, though she wouldn't have said it was her favorite thing in the whole world. Maybe she and Violet should make something out of felt instead of pinecones. But it was probably too late, if Violet and her mother had already gathered three hundred of them.

Across the playground, she saw Julia and Kelsey giggling together. Were they laughing at her? At her dad? Or at some private hilarity having to do with Frizzy Fred and his antics? Either way, the sight of their shared amusement made her heart ache.

"I'll have my mother get us some glue and glitter," Amy said briskly. "I've got to go now. See you later, Violet."

Violet's eyes filled. But Violet couldn't really expect that Amy would spend every free minute with her just because they were dumping glitter on pinecones together, could she?

When Amy reached Julia and Kelsey, their giggling stopped. A bad sign. Amy pretended not to notice. She had been avoiding Julia and Kelsey ever since the horrible apple-crisp afternoon almost a week ago. But now she had to try to make things right.

"Hi, you two! Do you want to do something after school today?"

"Well . . ." Julia said.

"It's just that . . ." Kelsey said.

Julia plunged ahead. "We really need to work on our Frizzy Freds. Each one takes almost five minutes to make, and we think we're going to need, like, hundreds."

"Our first selling session isn't till next week," Amy pointed out.

"Yes, but . . ." Kelsey said.

Amy didn't know why she was begging them. But she just wished desperately that everything between them could be the way it was before, Violet or no Violet, Frizzy Fred or no Frizzy Fred, Dad or no Dad.

"Oh, come on," Amy said, forcing a light, friendly laugh. "You can make Freds anytime."

There was a long pause.

"If we go to your house, is your father going to be there?" Julia asked.

The question felt like a fist in Amy's stomach. Even though she knew the answer, Amy asked, "Why?"

"Well, you know. He's just kind of—well, I mean, it's kind of strange. How he doesn't work anymore. And hangs around the house." Julia looked sorry she had said anything, but there was no way she could take the words back once they had been spoken. "Well, isn't it?"

Amy turned and walked away. She waited to see if Julia and Kelsey would come running after her. They didn't.

Violet was still standing alone, at the spot where Amy had left her.

"Do you want to come over today?" Amy demanded fiercely.

Violet's face lit up. "To your house?"

"We won't have those—whatever you called them. Hors d'oeuvres. But we can make something ourselves. Popcorn and apples. We can stop by your house on the way home and get some pinecones to start on. I think we have leftover glitter and glue somewhere. My mother can get us some more."

Amy was talking fast so she wouldn't cry. Wouldn't that be a sight, Amy and Violet, Mini-Society partners, standing on the Riverside Elementary School playground, bawling together.

"Do you really mean it?"

"Of course I do." Amy kept on talking. "We can probably get fifty pinecones done today. And then another fifty tomorrow."

She and Violet were going to sell all three hundred sticky, glittery pinecones, or die trying.

. . .

Amy could tell that Violet had never sprinkled glitter on a glue-covered pinecone before, at least not without her mother supervising every shake of the glitter tube.

"It doesn't matter if it's exactly even," Amy said, trying to keep the impatience out of her voice. Violet was still fussing over her third pinecone; Amy had done at least twenty.

"Well, we want people to buy them, don't we?" Violet asked. She sounded perilously close to tears.

"People aren't going to be counting how many glitter specks are on each one." What Amy really wanted to say was: *People aren't going to buy these, anyway.* But she knew better than to say that to Violet.

How *would* you make people buy sticky, glittery pinecones?

"We need to come up with some kind of name for them," Amy said.

"That's a good idea," Amy's dad said, joining the conversation.

She and Violet were sitting at the kitchen table, while Amy's father—her father!—was making dinner. From thirty-minute curried chicken breasts he had gone on to make thirty-minute apricot-glazed pork chops and thirty-minute hamburger stroganoff. Tonight was going to be thirty-minute Moroccan lamb with couscous.

"I think it's so cool that your dad cooks," Violet said. "My dad can't make anything. Of course, it's not like my mom would let him. She's kind of particular about things in the kitchen. I can't even open a package of cookies without her saying, 'Oh, I can do that for you, honey.' "

Amy didn't comment. Some things were too complicated to explain. She was mainly glad that her dad was dressed and shaved and acting like a normal father.

"So what can we call them?" Amy asked. "We need another word that starts with *P*. Pretty Pinecones. No. Perfect Pinecones. No." Pathetic Pinecones?

"Why does it have to start with *P*?"

"It's called alliteration, when two words start with the same letter. It sounds good. Like Isaiah's project: Crayon Critters. Doesn't that sound better than Crayon Animals?"

"But it doesn't have to be a *P*," Violet said. "We don't have to call them pinecones at all. We could call them Divine Decorations. Or Glittery something. Glittery Glamour Cones?"

*Not* Glittery Glamour Cones.

"Divine Decorations doesn't sound so bad," Amy said. "Dad, would you buy something called Divine Decorations?"

Her father looked up from the stove. "This couscous is incredible stuff. It cooks in *five* minutes, did you know that? And there are so many different things you can do with it. I'm surprised nobody's come up with a five-minute recipe book all based on couscous."

Then he paused and repeated Amy's question. "Would I buy something called Divine Decorations? Do you want an honest answer?"

Amy shot him a warning look. She blinked her eyes emphatically a couple of times, hoping he would get the connection: eyes, tears, don't get Violet started!

"I think it's a catchy name," he said slowly. "It's just that I'm not big on decorations myself. Your mother—Amy's mother—is the one who likes to decorate. But I think if someone *did* like to decorate, then, yes, Divine Decorations would be just the thing."

"Okay," Amy said to Violet. "Divine Decorations it is. We need to sell three hundred Divine Decorations."

"Do you think kids in our class like to decorate?" Violet's voice had an ominous wobble in it.

No. And if they did, they wouldn't want to decorate with pinecones, however divine.

"We have to make them *want* to decorate!" Amy said firmly.

"Advertising," her father said. "That's what advertisers do all the time. Convince you that you desperately need something that you never even heard of three minutes ago."

"How do they do it?" Amy asked.

"They prey on people's fears and insecurities. They make you think you smell bad, so they can sell you deodorant. Or that you'll be disgraced for life if your shirt collars aren't dazzlingly white. So they can sell you laundry detergent with bleach and brighteners."

"I guess fifth graders have a lot of fears and insecurities," Amy said, starting a list in her head already.

"I *know* fifth graders have a lot of fears and insecurities," Violet said. Violet probably had the list memorized.

Violet had even been afraid of Wiggy. She had taken one look at poor old Wiggy and shrieked with pure terror. So Wiggy was out in the backyard now, waiting patiently to come back in. But instead of padding around the yard looking for old buried bones, Wiggy was lying in the sunlight, dozing. Amy hoped she wasn't sick.

Amy thought for a moment about her own fears and insecurities. Would Wiggy get older and older and finally die? Would her father find another job? Would her parents stop fighting? Would Todd fail Mini-Society because he refused to come up with a product? Would she ever be friends with Julia and Kelsey again? Did she *want* to be friends with Julia and Kelsey again?

Not a single one had anything to do with decorated pinecones.

Ten minutes later, as the smell of the Moroccan lamb was starting to make Amy's mouth water, she and Violet had their ad.

*Do you feel bored and blah?*
*Is your life dull and dreary?*
*You need **Divine Decorations**!*
*Add some excitement to your decor.*
*Glitter!*
*Glamour!*
*The perfect pinecone is waiting for you.*
*Just 20 minis each.*
*Get them while they last!*

Amy was pleased that she had the alliteration of *bored* and *blah, dull* and *dreary, glitter* and *glamour, perfect* and *pinecone*. And when she typed it up on the computer, she could make each line print in a different color. She could even sprinkle a bit of glitter on each ad. She couldn't believe anyone else would think of creating an ad for their product.

Maybe she and Violet could sell three hundred pinecones, after all.

"Clear off the table, girls. It's time for dinner," Amy's father said. He hesitated. "Violet, why don't you call your parents and ask if you can stay."

Amy would have shot him an angry look, if she hadn't been afraid Violet would see it. She didn't want her strange father issuing invitations to her strange friends—strange not-even-friends—to eat his strange meals, even though so far the meals had turned out to be surprisingly good. But Violet was already racing eagerly to the kitchen phone.

"I don't want anyone to miss out on Moroccan lamb with couscous!" Amy's dad said.

Amy couldn't stay angry. Her dad and Violet both looked so happy that Amy started to let herself hope that maybe Divine Decorations *were* the secret to happiness.

9

**I**s something wrong, Todd?" Ms. Ives had asked Todd the other day, when she realized that he didn't have a product idea for the first Mini-Society selling session.

Well, yes, something in Todd's life was wrong.

Every single thing in Todd's life was wrong.

Todd couldn't figure out why he had developed such a block against making a product for Mini-Society. Most of the products people had come up with were nothing great. An autograph book made of squares of different-colored construction paper stapled together. Beaded bracelets. Little plastic bags of hot cocoa mix with a few rock-hard mini-marshmallows. Todd could come up with something as good as that—if not better.

The problem was that everyone expected him to come up with something terrific: Todd the inventor, Todd the me-chanical genius, Todd the engineer. It was hard trying to live up to other people's expectations. And the engineers in his family weren't doing so hot lately.

And then, that Saturday, Todd's soccer team lost. They had been undefeated for almost two entire years, and now they lost, 3–2, to a team they had beaten 4–1 the year before. There were at least three moments in the game when, if

Todd had done something different, his team might have won: when he slipped on the wet grass and fell down; when he rushed and missed a goal in the first period; when a foul was called on him, giving the other team a free kick.

Damon's dad tried to keep a positive tone as he talked with the guys on the field afterward, even though Todd knew that the coach minded the loss even more than the players did. "Every team loses sometimes," Damon's dad told them.

That was true of every *other* team. But teams with Damon on them weren't supposed to lose.

"You can tell what a team is made of," Damon's dad continued, "by what they do *after* they lose. Do they blame the other team, criticize the refs, sulk, whine, give up? Or do they accept full responsibility for the loss, learn from it, and play their hearts out for the rest of the season?"

Todd had no intention of blaming the other team or criticizing the refs. But sulking, whining, and giving up had a certain appeal.

And *then*, just when Todd thought with some grim satisfaction that his life had finally reached bottom, something happened that was worse than Mini-Society, and the flubbed soccer game, and his father's unemployment, and his parents' quarrels all put together.

Saturday, after the game, when Todd went to hang up his jacket on the pegs by the kitchen door, he saw that Wiggy's bowl from breakfast was untouched. Wiggy always ate every last speck of dog food, as if her mother had taught her to clean her plate. And when Wiggy cleaned a plate, she *cleaned* it, licking it bare, polishing it with her smooth pink tongue until it was positively gleaming.

Her food bowl was full, and she hadn't touched her water bowl, either.

"Wiggy!" Todd called, hoping she'd come padding down the stairs to greet him, a bit stiffly no doubt, but still with her tail wagging as hard as it could. Wiggy might have some arthritis in her legs, but so far there was no sign of arthritis in her tail.

"Wiggy!" Todd called again, more softly this time. He wanted to be able to let himself pretend that the only reason Wiggy wasn't coming was that she hadn't heard.

He finally found her lying listlessly on the floor beside his bed. His stomach clenched with fear. Still, he had a secret moment of gladness that she had come to his room when something was wrong. The whole family loved Wiggy, but Todd loved her the most. Down deep, he thought of her as *his* dog.

"Wiggins," he whispered. She gave him a pleading look with her glassy eyes. "Wiggins, what is it?"

Wiggy gave one feeble thump of her tail.

"Dad!" Todd shouted at the top of his lungs. "Dad!"

Amy came running first.

"Wiggy's sick. I think . . ." He swallowed hard. "She's very sick."

Amy took one glance at Wiggy's still body, and her face crumpled. "Oh, Wiggy!" Amy knelt down by Wiggy's side, patting her gently and crying at the same time.

Todd wished he could do that, too. He'd never been able

to cry. It wasn't that his parents had ever told him not to cry. Damon's dad had once told some guy on the soccer team, who was in tears after a missed goal, that crying was for girls. Todd's parents would never say anything like that. It was more that his tear ducts didn't work right, or something. Maybe that was Violet's problem, too, only the other way. Her tear ducts worked overtime. Todd's tear ducts didn't work at all. But his eyes burned with the tears he couldn't shed.

Their father appeared in the doorway. "What's wrong?"

"It's Wiggy," Todd managed to say.

Amy lifted her wet face from Wiggy's fur so their father could examine her. "We'd better take her to the vet," he said. "I'll call Dr. Atriya and tell him we're coming."

He laid one hand on Todd's shoulder, the other on Amy's. "Wiggy is an old dog," he said gently. "She's an old dog who's had a long, wonderful life." Then he stooped and hoisted Wiggy's limp body and carried her down to the car, Todd and Amy following behind him.

．　．　．

Dr. Atriya was a soft-voiced, dark-skinned, kindly man. After examining Wiggy, he said that she had an infection, sort of like the flu in human beings. He gave her a shot of medicine; Wiggy didn't even seem to notice the shot.

"I need to keep Wiggy here at the pet hospital a few days for observation," Dr. Atriya said. "But she can go home as soon as the medication starts to take effect."

Todd was feeling a little more hopeful, even though Dr. Atriya hadn't promised them that Wiggy would be all right.

But then Dr. Atriya said, "Fourteen is old for a dog like Wiggy."

It was almost the same thing their father had said. Todd knew they were both trying to prepare him and Amy for the idea that Wiggy might die. But nothing could prepare him for that. Nothing.

When they were home again, their father called their mother at work to tell her what had happened.

"I'm going to go upstairs and write a poem for Wiggy," Amy said. "That's the only thing that helps when you feel this way: writing a poem."

Writing a poem might help Amy when she felt this way. It wouldn't help Todd.

Todd went to his room and lay on his bed, staring at the braided rug where he had found Wiggy two hours before. He had never given any thought to the rug, but now, in Todd's mind, it was the place where Wiggy wasn't. He thought he saw a couple of her graying dog hairs there and leaned over the side of the bed to look more closely. Yes, there they were: three wispy white hairs on the brown-and-red braided strands of the rug.

It felt like something Amy might write a poem about. But Wiggy hadn't been lying on the floor beside Amy's bed; she had been lying on the floor beside Todd's. If anyone was going to write a poem about Wiggy's rug, it would have to be Todd.

Todd had never written a poem before, just to write one. He had written poems for school assignments. The easiest poems were haiku, because they were the shortest, only seventeen syllables each. If you had to write a poem, the shorter the better. Plus, counting out the syllables—five, seven, five—made writing a poem feel almost like solving a math problem.

On his desk Todd found a blank page in his math notebook and a too-short number-two pencil. He stared at the paper and thought for a moment. Then he started to write.

HAIKU FOR WIGGY (MY DOG) IN THE PET HOSPITAL

*The rug by my bed*
*Is empty now, where she used*
*To lie next to me.*

*I miss my Wiggy.*
*I wish I could feel the touch*
*Of her soft wet tongue.*

*I miss my Wiggy.*
*I wish I could hear the thump*
*Of her wagging tail.*

*Three hairs from her fur*
*Are all that is here right now.*
*Three little white hairs.*

Then something strange happened. Todd dropped the notebook and his stubby pencil onto the floor at the side of his bed, and he cried.

．　．　．

That evening, after dinner (thirty-minute Korean chicken thighs, made by his father), Todd went back downstairs to ask his parents if they could call Dr. Atriya to find out how Wiggy was doing. He stopped outside the kitchen door when he heard the low, intense murmur of their voices. It sounded as if they were having an important conversation.

Had Ms. Ives called them about his Mini-Society product? Was his dad telling his mom about the lost soccer game? Could they possibly have heard him crying in his room over Wiggy?

Todd knew he shouldn't listen, but he couldn't help himself. He caught his mother's voice first.

". . . don't know when I've been more worried about her."

"Well, she's always been so attached to Wiggy. I remember her toddling around the family room, clinging to Wiggy's fur. We're lucky Wiggy was always such a patient dog."

"And this falling out with Julia and Kelsey. Has she said anything to you about it?"

"No. I gather once she got stuck with Violet as her Mini-Society partner, they both just decided to drop her."

There was a pause. "Girls can be so cruel sometimes," his mother said, her voice tight and bitter. "I don't know how any girl survives adolescence unscathed."

"I have a terrible feeling this Mini-Society thing is going to turn out to be a disaster. You know, those pinecones of

Amy's. I don't think our Amy is cut out to be an entrepreneur."

"What is Todd making?"

"He hasn't mentioned it. Knowing Todd, it's something clever, sensible, and efficient, which will probably earn him a small fortune. I know it's hard for Amy sometimes, when Todd is so successful at almost everything."

"If anything happens to Wiggy . . ." his mother said.

"One of these days something *is* going to happen to Wiggy."

"I just hope it isn't now. For Amy's sake. Todd is so much better at weathering disappointments, taking them in his stride. All I can say is, it's a relief to have one we don't have to worry so much about."

Todd slipped upstairs, without asking his question.

It was amazing, absolutely amazing, what parents didn't know.

**O**n the morning of the first Mini-Society selling session, Amy and Violet went into the classroom before the bell rang and left a Divine Decorations ad on every desk. The first Mini-Society selling session was for their class only. Then they'd have an "international" selling session for all the fifth graders, and parents, too.

The ads had turned out even better than Amy had hoped. She had printed them in colored ink, and drawn a little pinecone on each one, and dusted it with glitter. Julia and Kelsey were going to wish they had thought of making ads for Frizzy Fred. Instead of glitter, they could have stuck on each one a wisp of Fred's pink hair.

But as soon as the others came streaming in from the playground, Amy could tell that the ads had not been a good idea, to put it mildly.

Some of the ads simply fell on the floor as kids took their chairs down from the tops of their desks. Nobody bothered to pick them up. Amy hated to think of all that painstakingly applied glitter being trampled by careless feet.

"Divine Decorations?" Amy heard someone ask. "That sounds dumb. Whose product is *this*?"

Well, she had thought it was dumb herself a week ago.

" 'The perfect pinecone is waiting for you,' " another boy read aloud. "I don't want any perfect pinecones waiting for me. Help! I'm being stalked by a perfect pinecone!" He raced across the room, clutching his throat and rolling his eyes in mock horror.

Several of the boys began folding their ads into paper airplanes and flying them toward the trash can. Most of the planes crashed before they reached their destination. One boy launched his toward the Mini-Society cardboard buildings. It hit the hospital.

Across the room, Todd folded his ad neatly and put it inside his desk. One thing about Todd: he never laughed at Amy when things went wrong. Amy knew he must feel almost as terrible about the ads as she did—unless he was too busy feeling terrible about his own product. The last Amy had heard—ten minutes ago—he had nothing. And of course they were both feeling terrible every minute of the day about Wiggy, who was still in the hospital. Dr. Atriya had called last night and said that Wiggy's condition continued to be "worrisome." As if Todd and Amy needed to be told to keep worrying.

Amy saw Julia study her ad intently and whisper something to Kelsey. Kelsey whispered something to Julia, and both girls burst into wild giggles.

Violet saw them laughing, too. Her eyes filled with her usual tears. One slid down the side of her nose.

Ms. Ives came into the room at the height of the commotion. A low-flying ad airplane narrowly missed her as she strode to her desk. "Boys and girls! What is going on here?"

"Someone put ads for their product on all the desks," Damon reported. His tone sounded carefully noncommittal. Amy knew Damon wanted to sound somewhat scornful, in case Ms. Ives said that leaving ads on desks was against school rules—but not too scornful, in case Ms. Ives said that leaving ads on desks was a brilliant strategy.

Ms. Ives picked up one of the ads that had fallen on the floor and read it silently. Amy waited for her response.

"What a wonderful idea!" This time Ms. Ives didn't make her comment into a question. Her face lit up with genuine enthusiasm. "Amy, Violet, you two are really getting into the spirit of our Mini-Society. Advertising is a big part of how products are sold in the real world."

Unfortunately, it didn't seem to be a big part of how products were sold in Mini-Society.

Or not sold. As the case might be.

.   .   .

At lunch Amy sat with Violet. It had been a long two weeks since she had sat with Julia and Kelsey. She hadn't even spoken to them since the day Julia had said that she didn't want to come to Amy's house if Amy's dad was there.

"The thing about ads?" Amy said to Violet, in a low voice. "When they *don't* work, they make your fears and insecurities even worse."

"Okay, the ads didn't work," Violet said. "But once people *see* the pinecones, they'll want them, don't you think?"

Amy took a deep breath. "Actually—no."

For once, Violet didn't cry. Maybe it was better to have a

bad truth said out loud than to keep on pretending that it wasn't true.

"What did your brother make?" Violet asked Amy.

There was no point in lying. "He didn't make anything."

Violet looked flabbergasted. It had probably never occurred to her that someone could simply refuse to do an assignment.

"Why not?"

"I don't know," Amy said, though suddenly she did, sort of. It was as if Todd couldn't succeed while their dad was failing. Or something like that. But the Divine Decorations weren't exactly going to be a huge success, either. Right now it looked as if they might be the biggest failure in the history of any Mini-Society selling session, in any school, anywhere.

.   .   .

After lunch, something about the classroom looked different. Amy looked again. A lot of the desks had signs taped to the front of them. The signs said NO SOLICITATIONS.

"What does NO SOLICITATIONS mean?" Violet asked in a voice that sounded as if she already knew.

"I think it means *no ads*," Amy said.

She was furious. She knew, she just knew, that the signs had been Julia's or Kelsey's idea: they were still giggling out by the water fountain. Amy snatched the sign from Julia's desk, and then from Kelsey's, crumpled each one into a hard little ball, and stuffed them into her own messy desk. Wordlessly, Violet started removing the signs from the other desks. Todd's desk didn't have one, of course, and neither did Isaiah's. The other kids, coming in from lunch recess, stared. Amy didn't care.

Ms. Ives, busy writing on the chalkboard, didn't seem to notice that anything was wrong. After calling the class to order, she explained the procedure for the first selling session. Students could buy goods with the minis they had earned from doing their classroom jobs over the past few weeks. They could also buy goods with the profits from their own sales. At the same time, they needed to save minis to invest in manufacturing more of their product for the international selling session.

"And remember, you may want to make a *different* product if you find that *this* product isn't selling as well as you had hoped," Ms. Ives said. At least she didn't look directly at Amy and Violet as she said it. She seemed to be trying very hard to look anywhere except at Amy and Violet.

There was more commotion as the students set up shop. Violet had brought in a pretty basket, lined with red felt, and it did look appealing with the Divine Decorations spilling out of it. Isaiah had cleverly arranged his Crayon Critters in a little stockyard made of Lincoln Logs. Julia and Kelsey had put on their own bright pink Frizzy Fred wigs. Damon had propped his calendars on the chalkboard ledge where the flag designs had been, twelve calendars, each opened to the picture for a different month. But all the pictures looked pretty much the same. It was bright and sunny almost every day in Colorado.

Todd's desk was bare.

Amy swallowed back a choking lump in her throat. Why couldn't he have made *something*? Anything. Even her pinecones were better than nothing. But last night when she had tried to talk to him about it, he had just turned away.

The selling began.

Todd bought the first pinecone. The only pinecone?

But Isaiah came by next. "I'll take two dozen," he announced.

"You're kidding," Amy said.

"No, he's not," Violet said quickly. "That will be four hundred eighty minis, please."

"Hey, I'm rich!" Isaiah said. "I have to spend my ten thousand minis on something."

Amy and Violet took turns selling while the other shopped. That was one advantage of working with a partner. Amy bought a crayon pig from Isaiah, and a paper flower from someone else, and some surprisingly tasty homemade fudge. She refused even to look at the Frizzy Freds. But she saw a lot of kids carrying them around. The matching wigs, she had to admit, had been a stroke of genius.

At the end of the session, Amy and Violet had sold twenty-six pinecones total. One to Todd, twenty-four to Isaiah, and one to Ms. Ives, who despite all her talk about not buying anything out of pity, had bought one item from everyone.

"I can't believe it!" Amy heard Kelsey squealing. "I mean, I knew everyone would love Fred, but I never dreamed we'd sell *this* many!"

Hot tears stung Amy's eyes. She tried to turn away before anyone could see.

But Violet had seen.

"Don't cry," she whispered to Amy.

*Violet* was telling *Amy* not to cry?

"It doesn't help," Violet said. "Take it from me."

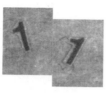

Todd felt Ms. Ives's eyes on him all Tuesday morning, so he wasn't surprised when she stopped by his desk just before recess and said, "Todd, I'd like to talk to you for a minute, please."

"Okay," Todd said, though he knew she was going to want *him* to do the talking, and it would take a lot longer than a minute.

Ms. Ives waited until the others had trooped noisily out of the room, and then she said, "Todd, we need to talk about what happened yesterday. Or rather, what didn't happen."

"I just couldn't think of anything," Todd said lamely.

Ms. Ives looked almost as miserable as Todd felt. "What's the matter? Is it something at home?"

Todd couldn't bear to tell her that his dad didn't work and his parents argued all the time. It felt like too much of a betrayal, to tell those things to people at school. And if he told Ms. Ives how old Wiggy was getting, and how sick she had been, and how she was still in the hospital, he might start to cry right there in the classroom. Todd had felt a lot safer back when his tear ducts had been broken. But he had to say something.

He took his math notebook from his desk and opened it

to the page with the poems about Wiggy. Ms. Ives accepted the notebook from him and read them through silently.

"These are beautiful!" she said. "I didn't know you wrote poetry. I thought Amy was the poet in your family."

Todd didn't reply. He hadn't let her read the poems to show off how great they were; he had let her read them so she'd know about Wiggy and stop bothering him about Mini-Society.

As if hearing his thoughts, Ms. Ives asked, "Is Wiggy all right now? Is she home from the pet hospital?"

"She's better. She's coming home tomorrow. But everyone keeps telling us"—Todd imitated the doctor's voice— " 'Wiggy is a very old dog. Wiggy has had a very good life.' As if that makes it all right that she might . . . " He couldn't say the word. He was glad Ms. Ives didn't say it, either.

"So this has been a hard time for you," Ms. Ives said awkwardly. "You've had a lot on your mind."

Poor Ms. Ives. She had only been teaching four weeks and had already had to deal with Isaiah's klutziness, Damon's smugness, Amy's messiness, and now a kid with a sick dog and an unemployed dad and a crabby mom and no Mini-Society product.

"But, Todd," she said. Todd had known her next sentence would have to start with *But*. "You still have to do your schoolwork. You still need to come up with a product for Mini-Society. You have almost two weeks until the second selling session."

"I know."

"Maybe I should talk with your parents?" Ms. Ives asked, as if unsure herself what to do next.

That was all his parents needed: a phone call from his teacher about problems at school, when they already had so many problems at home.

"Please don't," Todd almost begged. "I'll come up with something for the next selling session. I promise."

"How about working with a friend? Most of your class-mates are working with partners already, but some are working alone and might be happy to have you join their business. What about Damon? I think he could use some help with his calendars."

Damon? But then Ms. Ives had thought it was a good idea to make Amy work with Violet.

Todd must have made a face without realizing it, be-cause Ms. Ives said quickly, "Or how about Isaiah? You two are good friends, aren't you? I think he has more orders for his Crayon Critters than he can handle."

"It wouldn't be fair," Todd said. "It was his great idea." To himself, he added: *I never let him share any of my great ideas, back when I had them.*

"It's fair if he has more work than he can do by himself. And if he really wants you to do it."

"Okay," Todd said. "Maybe I'll ask him." *Maybe.*

"Good! Oh, and, Todd? Would you be willing to give me a copy of the poems you just shared with me? I'd like to—"

Todd didn't wait for her to finish. The whole conversa-tion had gone on too long already. He tore the paper out of his spiral notebook and handed it to Ms. Ives. "Here, keep it. Do whatever you want with it."

"But then you won't have a copy."

"I don't need one."

He didn't need a bunch of poems about Wiggy. He needed Wiggy.

. . .

Todd had told Ms. Ives that maybe he would ask Isaiah about becoming his partner in Crayon Critters. He hadn't said he'd definitely do it. Maybe always included the possibility of maybe not.

The problem was, he didn't even know *how* to ask Isaiah. *Um . . . Isaiah? Now that you finally have a great idea for something, and I have no idea at all, do you want to be partners?* He knew what he'd say if he were Isaiah: *I've decided I want to work alone.* The answer didn't seem as simple and straightforward when he imagined someone else saying it to him.

At lunch Todd and Isaiah were leaving the cafeteria line with their trays loaded with macaroni and cheese, green beans, apple turnovers, and milk, when Isaiah dropped his halfway to their table. It fell to the floor with a crash, and everyone in the cafeteria stopped talking mid-sentence to burst into cheers. It was always an event when someone dropped a tray, even though Isaiah dropped his once every few weeks.

The lunchroom lady was upon them instantly, surveying the wreckage. However bad the cafeteria macaroni and cheese looked on the tray, it looked even worse on the floor.

"Isaiah," the lunchroom lady said with a sigh. She was new to the school, like Ms. Ives, but she already knew Isaiah's name. "What are we going to do with you?"

Isaiah made an appropriately contrite face. Todd knew Isaiah really did feel terrible whenever he made a big mess for Frank, the school custodian, to clean up. Frank joked that he might retire when Isaiah graduated from fifth grade at the end of the year, because there would no longer be enough work for him at Riverside Elementary.

The lunchroom lady got a new tray for Isaiah and even carried it to the table for him. Apparently she didn't want to risk two crashes in five minutes.

"You never drop *your* tray," Isaiah said to Todd ruefully.

Todd shrugged. "I messed up three times at the soccer game last week. I got two wrong on the last spelling test. I couldn't think of anything to make for Mini-Society."

"Yeah," Isaiah said, looking grateful for Todd's list of his own mistakes. "I guess everyone messes up sometimes."

Todd considered that. He felt as if he had gone from being a person who never messed up to a person who always messed up.

"How's Crayon Critters doing these days?" Todd asked. He hoped it didn't sound too much like a hint.

"Great. I have, like, ten orders already for the next selling session. Two pigs, two sheep, and six chickens. The chicken is turning out to be my best seller. Because of the flag, I guess. Now that people know what the chicken stands for, everyone wants one. It's good to stand for something."

Todd swallowed hard. "You don't—you don't need an assistant or anything, do you?"

A huge grin spread across Isaiah's face. "You mean—you? I didn't think you liked working with other people."

"Oh, forget it," Todd said roughly. He couldn't go through with it, not after all the times he had let Isaiah fail at something all by himself.

"I don't want to forget it! Of course I want to work with you."

"It's just not fair. I never shared my ideas with you. Why should you share your ideas with me?"

Isaiah's grin returned. "You never had an idea as terrific as this! An idea this terrific needs to be shared. I'll start— what are they called? Franchises. Like McDonald's. You can be my first Crayon Critter franchise. I'll franchise out—the pig. You can do all the pigs. And the sheep and cows, too. I'll be the chicken man, and you can do the rest."

Todd was afraid he might cry again, this time from sheer, dumb relief and happiness. Isaiah was definitely the best friend in the entire world. Instead, he slapped Isaiah on the back. "What if we run out of broken crayons?"

"Don't worry. My sister can break crayons as fast as I can drop trays. She's a crayon-breaking machine. I should probably put her on the payroll, but it's not like it's work for her to break them or anything. For her, breaking crayons comes naturally."

Todd returned Isaiah's grin.

"So we're in Crayon Critters together," Isaiah said.

"We're in Crayon Critters together," Todd agreed.

· · ·

Until Todd became Isaiah's assistant, he had never real- ized how satisfying it could be to pour melted crayon bits into pig-shaped molds and watch them harden into their new form. If one of the Critters didn't turn out, he could melt it and start over again. A failed pig could become a successful sheep. A failed sheep could become a successful cow. And all of them could become successful chickens.

"I'm too rich," Isaiah complained to Todd. They were in Isaiah's kitchen after school, melting a new batch of crayons under the watchful eye of Isaiah's mother. She wanted to make sure there were no accidents with the hot wax. For some reason, she seemed to expect one.

"There's no such thing as being too rich," Todd said. "Is there?" If so, it certainly wasn't a problem his family had to worry about lately.

"Sure there is. Look at the world. Half the people in it are too rich, and the other half are too poor. Well, not half. I heard somewhere, it's like one percent are too rich, and the other ninety-nine percent are too poor. Or something like that. I'm the one percent who's too rich."

"People didn't have to vote for the chicken flag."

"Yeah, but I didn't have to charge ten thousand minis for it, either. I got carried away. I never thought I'd win."

Isaiah's mother pronounced the wax ready for pouring. "I know parents aren't supposed to help in Mini-Society," she said, "but it isn't really helping to make sure your son doesn't pour scalding wax all over himself, his sister, and his friend. And my stove. And my kitchen floor."

"I can do it," Todd offered. He wanted to be a true partner in Crayon Critters and do his fair share of the work.

"Okay," Isaiah's mother said doubtfully.

Todd picked up the pot and started pouring. It was definitely tricky to pour the melted wax without spattering it. There had to be a better method.

"I'm going to give my money away," Isaiah said.

Todd almost dropped the hot, heavy pot. "You're kidding!"

"I'll give some to everyone in the class. Just split it up into twenty-five parts and let everyone have some."

"You're going to give your money to *Damon*?"

"Why not? I don't need it. That's sort of the point of the chicken flag. A chicken in every pot."

"I don't think Ms. Ives'll let you do it. Isn't the point of Mini-Society to get as rich as you can?"

"I already did that."

"You're nuts," Todd informed him. But he'd like the world a whole lot better if everyone in it were as nutty as Isaiah.

"Can I have some money, too?" Isaiah's little sister, Janie, asked, looking up from the floor, where she was coloring. Todd saw that she had broken another half-dozen crayons already.

"Of course you can," Isaiah told her. "Everyone can have some."

Todd wished it were real money, money that he could use at home to help his parents pay their bills. But right now Mini-Society money was better than nothing. And being Isaiah's assistant in Crayon Critters was better than nothing, too.

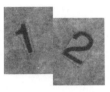

$A$my sat at her desk at school, trying to find her colored pencils. She wanted to make a card for Wiggy, who was coming home from the hospital today.

She had had a whole set of twenty-four brand-new colored pencils when school started nearly five weeks ago, and now all she could find was light blue, brown, purple, and yellow. There must be twenty other pencils in the desk somewhere, but it was impossible to find them.

A few weeks into every school year, her teacher would take one look at Amy's desk and say, "Trying to find anything in *your* desk, Amy, would be like trying to find a needle in a haystack."

As the rest of the class filed out for morning recess, Ms. Ives stopped by Amy's desk.

"I can't find the rest of my colored pencils," Amy told her.

Ms. Ives leaned over the desk. "How can you find anything at all in that desk? Trying to find a pencil in *your* desk, Amy, would be like—"

"Trying to find a needle in a haystack," Amy finished wearily. She was tired of needles, tired of haystacks. She was tired of having a messy desk.

"You've heard that line before, I take it?" Ms. Ives asked. Amy forced a smile.

"Okay, Amy, I have an idea. During recess today you and I are going to clean this desk."

If there was one thing Amy didn't want, it was Ms. Ives helping to clean her desk: seeing her poems, her scraps of paper with all her secret thoughts, the gum wrappers from the gum she wasn't even supposed to be chewing in class.

"I can do it by myself," Amy protested.

Ms. Ives looked dubious. Amy didn't blame her. She wasn't at all sure she could do it by herself.

"I'll help her," Violet piped up. "My mother always helps me clean my room. I'm great at cleaning."

"You don't want to miss recess, too, do you?" Ms. Ives asked her.

"I hate recess," Violet said. Violet's voice started to wobble on the last word, and her eyes filled with her usual reservoir of tears.

"Oh," Ms. Ives said. She clearly didn't know what to say next.

Not too long ago, Amy also hadn't known what to say when Violet came out with a statement like that. Now she just ignored it and moved on quickly to a happier thought.

Apparently Ms. Ives was learning, too. "Well, in that case . . . Okay, girls, good luck!" she finished brightly. Then she returned to her desk, and the two girls were left alone.

"Where do we start?" Amy asked. The job really looked hopeless.

Violet pulled a trash can, a recycling bin, and an empty

plastic crate over to the side of the desk. "First we take everything out. Everything. Just dump it on the floor. And then everything goes either *here*"—she pointed to the trash can—"or *here*." She pointed to the recycling bin. "Or it goes in this box, to be carried off where it belongs." She pointed to the plastic crate. "Or back in the desk."

Amy stared at Violet in awe. This was hardly the girl who couldn't sprinkle glitter on a pinecone without someone to tell her how many glitter specks to put on each little scale.

Violet scooped up a handful of plastic wrappers. "These go in the trash. They should have gone there in the first place. This library book. Are you finished reading it?"

Amy nodded. Violet placed it in the plastic crate.

"Your math notebook. Your social studies notebook. We'll start a *neat* pile for notebooks here on the left side of your desk."

Violet held up two crumpled paper balls. "What are these?"

Amy tried to remember. "Oh, the NO SOLICITATIONS signs."

"You saved *those*?"

Why *had* she saved them? "They're sort of like evidence, like proof."

"Proof of what?"

"Proof that Julia and Kelsey and I aren't friends anymore. Probably we never were friends. Not real friends."

Amy opened the two crumpled balls and smoothed them out. The two signs looked exactly the same, even though she was sure Julia had made one and Kelsey had made the other. Even though Julia was tall and Kelsey was short, and Julia had long blond hair and Kelsey had brown pigtails, they now seemed to her identical in almost every single way. They were more like twins than she and Todd were.

From the dwindling heap on the floor, Amy retrieved a note Julia had sent her:

*Hi, Amy! What do you think of Tanya's hair?*
$\heartsuit$ *Julia*

And a note Kelsey had sent her:

*Hi, Amy! Can you believe Randi's new shoes?*
$\heartsuit$ *Kelsey*

"Look at these," Amy said to Violet.

Violet read the notes. "Um . . . is there something interesting that I'm supposed to be noticing?"

"Look at their handwriting."

"It's neat. It's round. They both put circles for the dots over their *i*'s. They look pretty much the same to me."

"That's what I mean," Amy said. "They look almost exactly the same. Here, write me a note on this piece of paper." Amy handed Violet a scrap of paper from the floor.

"What should it say?"

"Anything. Try: 'Hi, Amy! What do you think of Frizzy Fred?' And then sign your name."

"I don't get it."

"Just do it."

Violet wrote the note and handed it to Amy.

"See? Your writing looks completely different from theirs. You write a lot smaller, like . . . like . . ."

"Like I don't want anybody to notice me," Violet finished.

"And your writing slants backward, like you're . . ."

"Afraid?"

Afraid even of Wiggy!

"Here, analyze mine." Amy scribbled the same sentence on a new piece of paper and thrust it at Violet. "What can you tell about me?"

Violet studied Amy's note for a few seconds. "You're messy." She looked down at the remaining heap on the floor, and both girls laughed. "But you're poetic, too."

"How can you tell I'm poetic? Are you just making that up?" Amy hoped her writing really showed that she was poetic.

"It's the way you make the capital *A* in Amy. Kind of like medieval writing, you know, extra large and flowery."

Amy felt the first stirrings of a wonderful idea.

"Are you girls cleaning Amy's desk or are you just gabbing?" Ms. Ives called over from the pile of papers she was grading.

"Neither!" Amy said triumphantly. "We've just discovered our new project for Mini-Society!"

Violet's face lit up. She really did look pretty when she was smiling.

"Handwriting analysis," Amy said. "For one hundred minis, we'll read your character from your handwriting. What do you think?"

Violet's newfound smile grew even wider. "For *two* hundred minis," Violet said.

· · ·

Wiggy was home! Amy sat beside her on the couch and held up her welcome-home card so Wiggy could see it. Amy had used twenty-three colored pencils—she and Violet had never found the twenty-fourth pencil, even after Amy's desk was completely clean, neat, and as organized as a desk could be. Sometimes, Amy had learned over the years, pencils just vanished.

Todd was playing Wiggy's favorite piece of music on the stereo: the *1812* Overture. At least, they thought it was her favorite piece of music, because she always thumped her tail during the cannon parts. She wasn't thumping her tail right now, but Amy knew Wiggy was glad to be back with the family who loved her.

Amy's father had made another terrific thirty-minute meal: chicken with white wine and tarragon. He had made dinner every night since he discovered the thirty-minute cookbook. And he had baked Wiggy a welcome-home cake: not a cake for Wiggy to eat herself, but one for the rest of them to eat in celebration.

"Did we have any chocolate cake mix?" Amy's mother asked him, sounding puzzled, as she took the first bite of the rich chocolate cake covered thickly with chocolate frosting.

"I didn't use a mix," he said.

"You baked it from scratch?"

"You follow the recipe. It wasn't hard. Just a lot of measuring and stirring. But it was all pretty straightforward."

"Will wonders never cease!" her mother said faintly. "If only . . ."

She didn't finish the sentence, but Amy knew she wanted to say: If only you could get a job and earn some money, too. Amy was glad she didn't say it. For a fleeting moment Amy wondered if her father could get a job making thirty-minute meals somewhere, but that was probably a silly idea.

"If only what?" her father asked sharply.

*Don't say it, don't say it, don't!*

"Nothing," her mother said. But Amy knew that her father knew exactly what her mother was thinking.

Then, as they were all scraping up their last crumbs of cake, Amy's mother turned to Amy. "Amy, I have a confession to make."

Amy stopped petting Wiggy. "What is it?" she asked.

"I borrowed your idea," her mother said.

"What idea?"

"Your idea about pinecones."

Amy wasn't in the mood to be teased about pinecones. "I never want to hear another word about pinecones as long as I live!"

But her mother's smile wasn't a teasing smile. "For the crafts class I'm going to be teaching at the store this Saturday, I thought we'd do all different kinds of crafts with pinecones. Everyone's yard is filled with them this time of year."

Todd looked as skeptical as Amy felt. "But, Mom," he began. Amy knew he wanted to warn her away from pinecones without coming right out and stating what a terrible failure the Divine Decorations had been. "Are you going to dip them in glue and glitter?" was all he said.

"Maybe. I thought the pinecones Amy made with Violet turned out real cute."

"Well, you're the only one who did," Amy snapped.

"With a narrow red velvet ribbon on them, for Christmas," their mother said dreamily, "they'd make lovely Christmas tree ornaments."

"I told you so," Todd said to Amy.

"Nobody bought any!" Amy shot back.

Their mother was evidently too absorbed to hear them. "And what about a pinecone bird feeder? Smeared with suet and sprinkled with birdseed and sunflower seeds? Great to hang on a tree branch right outside a window. Or pinecone wreaths?"

She was clearly on a roll now, envisioning an endless stream of pinecone creations.

"Pinecones glued to a Styrofoam core and then shellacked. Lovely on a front door or as a seasonal centerpiece. A plain unfinished wooden box could be transformed into a pinecone treasure chest. Tiny pinecones could work as earrings."

"Mom," Amy said, interrupting her reverie, "nobody I know wants to wear pinecone earrings."

"Maybe you and I know different people."

If her mother knew people who wanted to wear

pinecone earrings, she definitely didn't know the people Amy knew.

"Wiggy," Amy demanded, "do you want to wear pinecone earrings? Thump your tail once for no, and twice for yes."

Wiggy thumped her tail three times.

"Thank you, Wiggy," their mother said. "Three times means Wiggy wants to wear pinecone earrings more than anything in the world."

Amy knew it meant that Wiggy was glad to be home again. But her mother would have to find out the truth about pinecones the hard way.

When Todd got home from Isaiah's after school on Thursday, Amy was sitting on the family room floor, surrounded by books. It wasn't unusual for Todd to see Amy lost in a book, but it was unusual to see her reading three at one time.

"Do we have something due at school?" he asked uneasily. They were doing a big project on myths and legends in language arts, but Todd didn't think they had to hand in anything for another couple of weeks.

"I'm learning about handwriting analysis. You know, how you can tell someone's personality just by looking at his handwriting. Here, write something for me, and I'll tell you all about yourself."

Todd made a scoffing noise. To him, it was another piece of fake science, like astrology or palm reading. Or feeling the bumps on a person's head. Todd had once read that back in the nineteenth century, people thought you could analyze someone's character by looking at the shape of his skull. Maybe you could tell by the shape of someone's skull whether he had been in a bicycle accident or fallen down the stairs when he was a baby, but Todd didn't think you could tell much else.

"You don't believe me."

"I didn't say that."

"When you're someone's twin, you don't have to say anything for her to know what you're thinking."

"That's why the whole thing is so bogus," Todd said. "You'll look at my handwriting and see everything that you already know from living with me for ten and a half years, plus the nine months before that."

"No, I won't. I'll just go by what the books say. I got three of them out of the library on my way home. You should read them. They're fascinating. Like, look at this one." Amy opened the closest book to a page full of signatures. "This is from a famous murderer. See the strange way he crosses the *t*'s in his name? That shows he's an outlaw. He thinks the rules don't apply to him."

"So everyone who crosses his *t*'s in a strange way is a potential murderer?"

"No, but don't you think it's interesting that a murderer wrote that way? Look at this one: it's three times bigger than anybody's else's. Do you think this person has a big ego or a small ego?"

"Okay, big, but—"

"She was a famous movie star. The more you learn about this stuff, the more sense it makes."

Either that, or the more weird *you* became. "What got you started on this?"

"Because this is—ta-dah!—our new Mini-Society project. Violet and I are going to analyze people's personalities from their handwriting."

As a science, handwriting analysis might be completely bogus, but as a Mini-Society project, it did sound brilliant.

"It's better than pinecones," Todd admitted, "but I guess we'd better not tell that to Mom." When Todd got home, the kitchen table had been entirely covered with pinecone creations, even pinecone pets with little felt ears, goggly eyes, and ribbon tails. The pinecone pets had actually been pretty cute. They might have given Crayon Critters a run for their money as a Mini-Society sales item.

"Let me practice on you," Amy said. "Copy this for me. In cursive."

Mildly curious now, Todd wrote the short paragraph Amy showed him on the piece of unlined paper she provided, and waited for her verdict.

"Your line spacing shows that you're logical and organized," Amy pronounced. "Your overall style is kind of bare and simplified. That shows you're realistic and objective. The way you close up all your *o*'s and *a*'s shows that you don't like to reveal much of yourself to others."

"I'm so glad I had my handwriting analyzed, Madame Amy! I never would have known any of this otherwise!"

"And," Amy said, suddenly sounding worried, "you're depressed."

"I'm depressed?"

"Your lines slope downward. That means you're depressed. Has your writing always looked this way?"

Todd didn't know. He had never studied the slope of his lines before.

"Are you depressed?" Amy asked then.

What should he say? "Well, sort of," he finally replied. "I mean, aren't you? With everything that's been going on around here? But listen, I still have math homework for tomorrow. I better go."

As he walked away, he knew Amy was watching him. He straightened his shoulders so she wouldn't think his back looked depressed, too. Halfway up the stairs, he ran his hand, once, quickly, over his head, feeling for any stray lumps or bumps. If the downward slope of his handwritten lines showed that he was depressed, there was no telling what the shape of his skull might show.

. . .

"Give your money away?" Ms. Ives asked Isaiah. At least, Todd thought, she hadn't been holding a full pot of melted crayon wax when he'd told her his plan. "But, Isaiah— I don't think—it isn't really—Mini-Society isn't going to teach everyone about economics if successful students start giving their money away to less successful ones."

"In real life, some people give their money away," Isaiah pointed out.

Ms. Ives hesitated. "Well, that's true. But, Isaiah, are you sure? Your flag design won our election fair and square, and your Crayon Critters have sold so well. Do you really want to give all your money away?"

"Not all of it. I'll keep some for myself. I just want to share it."

Todd could see the wheels turning inside the teacher's

head. Was this the way Mini-Society was supposed to work, or not? Then her face cleared. "All right. You can be our Mini-Society's first philanthropist."

"What's a philanthropist?" Isaiah asked.

"The word literally means someone who loves his fellow man, or human beings. Someone who shares his wealth with others."

Isaiah gave a big smile. "That sounds like me."

"All right," Ms. Ives said again, as if to convince herself she had made the right decision. Todd thought she had. After all, it was Isaiah's money. What good was money if you couldn't do what you wanted with it, including giving it away?

"I'll make an announcement," Ms. Ives said. "Class!" She definitely sounded more confident than she had a few weeks ago. She hardly ever ended her sentences with question marks now, except when something really unusual happened, like the richest person in the class deciding to give his money away.

"Isaiah has just informed me that he wants to share some of his money with the rest of the class. This isn't part of the Mini-Society curriculum, but I've decided to let him do this if it's what he really wants."

"I did the long division," Isaiah said. "If I divide ten thousand minis twenty-five ways, you'll each get four hundred minis."

Everyone cheered. "Can we get it now?" someone asked.

"Isaiah?" Ms. Ives asked him.

"Come and get it!"

There was a stampede as the whole class crowded around Isaiah's desk to get their four hundred minis. Todd could tell from watching Ms. Ives's face that she was sorry she had allowed so much class time to be taken up with having Isaiah count out four hundred minis for every single student, but it was too late to stop the process.

Finally all the students were back in their seats again. Isaiah was beaming. And if Isaiah kept on earning heaps of minis by selling Crayon Critters with his new assistant, Todd knew that Isaiah would be giving away even more.

. . .

That night, as Todd's dad was making dinner (curried shrimp with basmati rice), Todd sat at the kitchen table doodling a design for a new Crayon Critter wax-pouring system. Pouring liquid wax from a full pot into little chicken molds was messy and dangerous. A funnel would give Todd more control over the flow of the wax, but he needed two hands to hold the heavy pot, and then someone else would have to hold the funnel and risk getting *his* hands spattered with hot wax.

What they needed was a pot with a built-in funnel—sort of like a teakettle, but with a removable lid. The lid would have to clamp on securely so that it wouldn't fall off during the pouring.

Todd felt his dad's eyes on his paper. "What're you working on?" his dad asked.

"I'm trying to help Isaiah with his Mini-Society business," Todd told him. He explained the problem about the pouring. He didn't tell his dad that he was Isaiah's official assistant in the business. He didn't want to hear how surprised his dad would be that he hadn't come up with any project of his own. But his dad was so lost in his own problems these days that he had never even asked Todd what he was making.

"I have some scrap metal down in the basement," his dad said. "We could probably weld something together after dinner. If you have time," his dad added, sounding suddenly tentative and hesitant.

"I have time," Todd said, trying not to sound too eager. This would be the first engineering project his dad had worked on since he lost his job.

When dinner was served, Todd hurried through the curried shrimp. He thought he had an idea for how to rig up the clamps.

"Where are you two off to?" Todd's mother asked as Todd and his father shoved back their chairs at the same moment and bolted toward the basement stairs.

"We're just fiddling with something," his dad said. Todd was grateful that his dad hadn't said more. He didn't like to talk about his ideas until he was pretty sure they were going to work out.

By the end of the evening, Todd and his father had the world's best wax-pouring contraption. Too bad Todd couldn't have a Mini-Society business of his own selling custom-designed wax-pouring devices. But he knew he'd have exactly one customer for that business. Even Amy wouldn't buy a custom-designed wax-pourer just to show Davidson family solidarity.

Still, there was nothing like dreaming up an idea and making a drawing of it and then building it, out of real solid metal that you could hold and touch, and watching it do exactly what you needed it to do.

Todd wondered if now his dad would feel even worse that he wasn't an engineer anymore. But his dad still *was* an engineer. You didn't have to have a job as an engineer to *be* an engineer. More than anything, though, Todd wished that his dad could find another job doing what he loved.

"That was fun," Todd said carefully.

"It sure was," his dad said. But he didn't say anything else.

"Come help me at the store today," Amy's mother urged her on Saturday morning. "I don't know if I can teach my first class without you."

"I haven't had such good luck with pinecones," Amy pointed out.

"Nonsense! Your Divine Decorations were lovely. They just weren't right for your classmates."

Amy tried to think of another reason for not spending her Saturday morning at the Crafts Cottage making things out of pinecones. "I'll miss Todd's soccer game."

This time a shadow crossed her mother's face. "Sometimes I wonder whether I've put too much pressure on Todd, all these years, making such a big deal out of attending every single game. Your dad can go."

"Wiggy might get sick again."

"Does this dog look sick to you?"

The contents of Wiggy's food bowl were vanishing at record speed. She was eating too fast to take time out to thump her tail at the mention of her name.

Amy couldn't think of a fourth excuse, so half an hour later she ended up in her mother's car on the way to the Crafts Cottage.

The class was held around a large table set up at the b of the store, where her mother had laid out a sample of each of the six projects the class would be making. The first thing Amy noticed was that the classroom was packed. All twelve seats at the table were taken by eager pinecone lovers.

Including Violet and her mother.

Violet waved enthusiastically at Amy. Amy found herself waving back just as enthusiastically. She had a sudden revelation: she *liked* Violet LaFarge. She liked Violet's quirky sense of humor and her genuine kindness. Even Violet's weepiness was sort of endearing once you got used to it. At least you never had to apologize when you were with Violet and felt like crying yourself.

Besides, Violet wasn't crying so much lately. There was the occasional sniffle, and a tear or two in the corner of her eye. But nothing that would really count as full-fledged crying.

The girls didn't have much time to talk, as the class was about to begin. But Amy did manage to whisper to Violet, "Aren't you tired of pinecones?"

"Tired of *pinecones*?" Violet asked incredulously. "I want to make those pinecone earrings. I think they're so cute, don't you?"

Amy had a vision of herself walking to class on Monday with Violet, each of them wearing a matching set of pinecone earrings. What would Julia and Kelsey say?

And then she had another revelation: she didn't care what Julia and Kelsey would say. But she didn't think she'd walk into class wearing pinecone earrings, anyway.

The class turned out to be lots of fun. It was odd watching her ordinary, everyday mother presiding over it, putting everyone at ease, explaining things in a way everybody could understand, helping people with their projects. The students in the class kept calling Amy's mother over to get her opinion on whether the shellac on their pinecone treasure boxes was too thick or too thin, and Amy marveled that they cared so much for the opinion of her mother.

"All my pinecones keep falling off!" Violet wailed.

"Here, honey, let me do it for you," Violet's mother said.

Amy's mother bustled over to them, glue gun in hand. "Violet can do it herself," she said, handing Violet the glue gun.

Violet stared at it as if it were a real gun. She turned large, frightened eyes toward her mother. But Amy's mother didn't yield. "Violet can do it herself," she repeated with a confident smile.

Five minutes later, Violet was staring at her finished pinecone treasure box in obvious amazement.

"I told you you could do it!" Amy's mother hurried off to help someone whose pinecone pets couldn't get the right cute expression on their pinecone faces.

Amy felt proud. Her mother was a good teacher. No, her mother was a *great* teacher.

"Here, Amy and Violet, you demonstrate this one," her mother said, pulling out a big bottle of glue and a huge jar of glitter. "I got the idea for these darling Christmas tree ornaments from a project the girls created themselves at school."

Amy was glad to let Violet do most of it. Violet's mother beamed at her, evidently thrilled to see her daughter hailed as a pinecone expert.

The red velvet ribbons added a lot to the overall effect. If Amy had to do it over again, she would market their pinecones as Christmas tree ornaments, after all. She and Violet could have hung the ornaments on a small fake Christmas tree set up on a desk, with a tape of Christmas carols playing softly next to it. Still, Amy was glad not to have to relive that particular event.

The women in the class actually squealed with excitement when her mother brought out the tiny pinecones for the earrings, the final item for the morning.

"My daughter-in-law is going to love these!" one woman exclaimed.

"I'm not giving *mine* away," another one said. "These are too cute for words!"

When the class was over, everyone was asking Amy's mother when the next one would be held, and what it would be on.

"Any ideas, girls?" her mother asked Amy and Violet.

"Felt," Violet said. "Do one on felt."

"Felt!" the women chorused.

"Felt it is," Amy's mother said happily. There was glitter on the side of her nose and a tiny scrap of red velvet ribbon caught in her hair, and dried glue everywhere. Amy hadn't seen her look so happy in a long, long time.

. . .

Todd's team had won that day. Amy knew as soon as she walked into the house with her mother and smelled frying bacon and heard the sizzle of pancake batter striking the hot griddle. Her father wouldn't have made a pancake and bacon brunch to console Todd for another loss; this had the smell and sound of a celebration.

To Amy's surprise, Damon and his dad were there, too.

"Run and check the bathroom!" Amy's mother whispered to her frantically. "Make sure it's okay!" Her mother hastily straightened the couch cushions in the family room and swept an untidy stack of newspapers out of sight as Amy made sure the downstairs bathroom was guestworthy, which it was. All would be well as long as Damon and his dad didn't ask for a tour of the upstairs.

"I thought the coach and the team's two stars deserved some of my famous victory pancakes," Amy's father said when she and her mother appeared in the kitchen.

To Amy's knowledge, her father had never made pancakes before in his life.

Amy saw her mother cringe at the jumble of dirty dishes in the sink, but at least they were in the sink and not strewn all over the counter. And the brunch smelled so good that no one was likely to think about the mess. It wasn't as if they were entertaining Violet's mother.

Amy helped her mother set the dining room table. She thought about looking for the cloth napkins they used on

Thanksgiving and trying to fold them into little tents, but then decided that paper napkins were fine. Her mother placed the sample pinecone wreath that she had brought home from the crafts class in the middle of the table as a centerpiece.

For the first part of the meal, everyone was too busy devouring pancakes and bacon to talk very much, but then the dads and the boys rehashed every minute of the game.

"I couldn't believe that pass you got off in the third quarter," Damon said to Todd.

"I couldn't believe it, either." Todd was beaming.

Amy wondered if Todd's handwriting would slope upward now.

Finally Damon's dad wiped his mouth with his napkin and pushed his chair back from the table. "We're going to have to wangle ourselves invitations to your house more often," he said. "Our meals have taken a dramatic turn for the worse since my company got a major new contract and Sheila's promotion came through."

"They're not so bad," Damon protested.

"If you like pizza on Monday, carryout Chinese on Tuesday, pizza on Wednesday, and carryout Chinese on Thursday."

"Who doesn't like that?" Damon asked.

As the grownups were saying their goodbyes at the front door, Damon said to Todd, "I hear you're in the Crayon Critter business now."

Todd shrugged. "Isaiah's making good money. He has more work than he can handle."

"Well, I just wanted to let you know that if little crayon lumps turn out not to be your thing, there's a place for you at Damon Enterprises. Remember the parent market. Calendars to send to all the relatives at Christmas. One for Uncle Sidney. One for Aunt Sally . . ."

"I'll think about it," Todd said.

Back in the dining room, the four of them worked together to clear the table.

"How did Mom's pinecone thing end up?" Todd asked Amy in a low voice.

"It was *fantastic*," Amy told him, amazed that she had almost forgotten about the morning's class in the excitement of the unexpected brunch. "Dad, you should have seen all the people at Mom's class today. They loved it! Everyone loved it. Max told Mom he wants her to teach a class every week."

Amy's mother blushed. "I got a raise, too. A *nice* raise."

Amy's dad put his arm around her and gave her a kiss on the cheek.

Amy sucked in her breath. She'd thought her parents didn't kiss anymore. "The moral of this," Amy concluded, "is never underestimate the power of pinecones."

Everyone laughed, but Amy saw Todd shoot a worried glance at their dad. What did he have to celebrate these days? Just a bunch of thirty-minute meals, a welcome-home cake for Wiggy, and some great pancakes. He still didn't have a job, or any prospects for getting one.

Suddenly Amy had an idea. She had to say it carefully so her father would be willing to listen.

"Dad?" She followed him to the kitchen, where he stood scraping dishes into the disposal, not that there was much to scrape of the delicious pancakes and bacon. "Those pancakes were *really* good."

"They were, weren't they? I may be an unemployed engineer, but I wield a mean spatula."

Luckily his tone was jovial, not bitter. He was giving her just the opening she needed. "Damon's dad said their meals are terrible. And our meals used to be terrible. I bet there are a lot of families with two working parents whose meals are terrible."

"Thirty-minute recipes," her father said cheerfully. "Must be a thousand of those."

"That's just *it*," Amy blurted out. "*You* could *make* thirty-minute meals for people. And sell them. For money. It's like we learned in Mini-Society. Supply and demand. There's a demand for good meals. And you could supply them."

Her father's pleased, self-congratulatory smile disappeared. "I'm an engineer, Amy, not a chef."

Todd and their mother had stopped wiping the counters and were watching them, obviously waiting to hear what Amy would say next.

She plunged ahead desperately. "In Mini-Society, we learned that if one thing isn't working out, you try another. Like the pinecones. They worked out great for Mom, but they didn't work out for Violet and me, so now we have a new project—where we analyze people's handwriting?—and it's going to be wonderful. I know it is."

Her father's face darkened. "Real life isn't exactly the

same as Mini-Society, Amy. Engineering to catering? That's quite a switch."

Amy held her ground. "Pinecones to handwriting analysis is quite a switch, too," she said, even though she knew it wasn't the same. She forced a confident smile.

But her dad didn't smile back. He slammed the dishwasher door shut and walked away.

**I** have an announcement to make," Ms. Ives said at the start of the day on Friday, once the class had finished the daily math challenge. Todd had gotten it right, as usual, but he hadn't bothered to raise his hand to share his answer with the class.

Ms. Ives gave Todd a meaningful look. Maybe the math team was going to have its first meeting of the year. Last year, Todd had been the top scorer on the team for the whole fourth grade. He didn't know if he would join the math team this year.

"My announcement," Ms. Ives said when the class had quieted down enough to listen, "is that one of your classmates has won the back-to-school poetry contest sponsored by our school district. Each teacher can submit poems from five students. I chose five students from this class, and one of you has won first prize in the upper-elementary division."

Everyone looked at Amy. Todd flashed her a big grin. She deserved it, both because she was a terrific poet—not that Todd was any judge of poetry—and because she had been through so much in the past few weeks, with her dumb friends Julia and Kelsey, and with old crybaby Violet and their failed pinecone business.

"First prize in the district's back-to-school poetry contest goes to Todd Davidson."

She must mean *Amy* Davidson.

"For his poetry 'Haiku for Wiggy.' "

Todd felt as if he had fallen hard on the soccer field, facedown, sprawling on the pounded dirt, all the wind knocked out of him. He wouldn't have given Ms. Ives a copy of his poems if he had known she'd send them to a contest. He vaguely remembered telling her she could do whatever she wanted with them, but he hadn't *meant* it. He had said it just because he felt so angry and despairing.

He didn't want to win a poetry contest. He wanted Amy to win. He wasn't a poet. This was the first poetry he had ever written of his own free will.

He tried to signal to Amy, but she was staring straight ahead, her face flushed a bright pink, smiling too hard, clapping for him with all her might.

"Can you read it to us?" someone asked.

"Todd? Would you like to read it, or do you want me to?" Ms. Ives held out the paper to him.

"I don't want to read it," Todd said dully.

"That's fine. I'll read it for you."

"I don't want you to read it, either."

"But, Todd—"

"It was *private*. I shouldn't have let you have it. It was *private*."

"Oh, Todd."

There was an uncomfortable silence in the classroom.

Todd blinked fiercely. This was the worst thing that had happened to him yet.

"Todd, I didn't mean— Todd, I'm so sorry."

"It's okay." If she would just stop talking about it, he could get through the rest of the day without breaking down.

"I think we should all be very proud of Todd," Ms. Ives said to the class. "Now get out your science folders, please."

Todd wondered if she would ask him to stay in during recess for another little chat and ask him again if anything was wrong at home. She didn't. For that he was grateful.

·  ·  ·

Todd had soccer practice after school, so he didn't have a chance to talk to Amy. Nothing he could have said would have helped, anyway. She already knew, from the scene that morning at school, that he hadn't wanted Ms. Ives to send his poem in to the contest. He couldn't very well apologize to her because the judges had thought his poem was better than hers.

Dinner that night wasn't a thirty-minute meal from the book. It was a Middle Eastern minted lamb and bulgur wheat casserole of his dad's own invention. Todd had to admit that Amy was right: if his dad wanted to try his hand at catering, he'd have some pretty delicious meals to make for his customers.

"Guess what?" Amy said. Her too-enthusiastic tone and overly wide smile warned Todd what she was going to say. He shook his head at her pleadingly, but she went on. "Ms.

Ives announced the winner of the district-wide back-to-school poetry contest today. The one she submitted my poetry to a couple of weeks ago."

"And you won? That's wonderful, honey!" Their mother obviously hadn't picked up on the slight tremor in Amy's voice.

"No, *Todd* won. Todd did! For poems he wrote about Wiggy."

"Todd?" Their mother stared at him.

He nodded grimly. He saw his mother's eyes dart nervously back and forth between him and Amy. "They weren't any good," he said. "The judges just picked them because everybody gets all choked up if you start telling them your dog is sick."

"My poem was about Wiggy being sick, too," Amy said.

For a long moment, no one said anything.

Finally their father said, "Well, that's wonderful! So what else happened today at school? What's going on in Mini-Society? Todd, I don't think you ever told us how your product turned out. We all had pinecones on the brain there for a while." He gave an awkward chuckle.

"I didn't have one." Todd was glad that he had something bad to tell them, to drive away their surprised, stricken smiles. "I couldn't think of anything."

"*You?*" his mother asked. "*You* couldn't think of anything?"

Todd didn't reply. He wasn't going to say it again.

"But, Todd—"

"Don't worry. I'm working with Isaiah in his business. I'm his assistant."

He knew his mother wanted to say, *You? You're Isaiah's assistant?* But she didn't.

"So everything's terrific now," Todd said. "You don't have to worry about me. You don't have to worry about me at all."

Suddenly he felt the minted lamb and bulgur wheat rise up in his throat. He swallowed it down.

"Todd," his father said gently, "why didn't you come to us for help if you were stuck for an idea?"

Now it was anger that was rising in Todd's throat, choking him, suffocating him, all the anger he had kept hidden lately.

"What ideas do you have? You don't have a job. You're not even looking for a job. You and Mom fight all the time."

He stared down at his plate, refusing to look at his father's face.

There was a long pause before his father spoke. "The economy is bad right now, Todd. You know that. I can't snap my fingers and make an engineering job appear. And the longer you're out of work, the more questions everyone has, about whether it's worth the risk to hire you."

"So maybe you're going to have to snap your fingers and make a different kind of job appear," Todd's mother said. Her voice, too, was tight with anger. "I made my job at the Crafts Cottage appear."

"So you want both of us to be working at the Crafts Cottage?" Todd's father asked. "You want both of us to be making puppets out of pinecones?"

"Are you making fun of my job?" His mother's voice was getting loud now.

"No, I'm simply pointing out that you and I are different people, with different tastes and talents."

"And I'm simply pointing out that we can't go on living on one Crafts Cottage salary forever. What's wrong with giving something else a try? What's wrong with at least trying Amy's catering suggestion until something else comes up?"

"I don't want you to try my suggestion!" Amy sounded close to tears. "I just want both of you to stop fighting!"

Todd caught a glimpse of Amy's face, pale and stricken. He couldn't bear it anymore. He got up from the table, ran upstairs to his room, and flung himself on his unmade bed. Wiggy padded after him.

Todd was afraid his mother would want to talk to him, but the soft knock he heard at his door a few minutes later was his dad's. "May I come in?"

Todd didn't say no, so his dad sat down on the edge of Todd's bed.

"I guess we didn't know how hard these past few weeks have been for you kids."

*You knew how hard they were for Amy,* Todd wanted to say.

"Amy shows her feelings more, but you—well, you don't. But I should have known. I guess we're all having to learn how to deal with the unexpected."

"That's why I like math," Todd said. "There isn't any unexpected."

"In engineering, there is. And you've always been our engineer. And now maybe you're our poet, too."

"I'm not a poet!"

"What's wrong with being a poet?"

"Amy's the poet."

"Maybe you're both poets. You're an engineer *and* a poet. With this new handwriting business of hers, Amy is an entrepreneur *and* a poet. Your mom is a homemaker, and now she's a teacher, too. And I . . ." Todd waited while his dad forced out the rest of the sentence. "Maybe I'm an engineer *and* a really terrific cook who might be able to make some money catering."

His dad reached over and gave Todd a hug. At first Todd resisted, but then he found himself hugging his father back, hard. When they finally let go, they each had tears in their eyes.

"Oh, Wiggy," Todd said after his father left the room. He hugged her even tighter than he had hugged his dad. She licked his hand and kept on licking it. Every lick washed away a little bit of his pain.

"*You* don't change, Wiggy." But even as Todd said it, he knew it wasn't true. Wiggy was growing old. Wiggy had been sick and could get sick again.

Everybody changed. But in some important ways, everybody also stayed the same. With Wiggy licking his hand, it felt all right somehow.

It felt all right.

There was an actual line in front of Amy and Violet's handwriting booth, a long line with both kids and adults in it. The sign on the booth said:

*Your handwriting reveals who you are!*
*Let us tell you the secrets of your soul*
*there in your handwriting*
*for all to see*
*200 minis*

Amy instructed the next customer, a girl from another class, how to produce a good sample of her handwriting—in ink, on unlined paper. Then Amy studied it. The girl had left narrow margins all around, which Amy now knew meant that the writer crammed her life with too many activities. The writing was very even in what the handwriting analysis books called its "baseline": even though the paper was un-lined, the writing moved across the page in perfectly straight lines. According to the books, that meant that the girl was focused on her goals.

She looked pleased with Amy's pronouncements. "That *is* what I'm like!" she said. "I made my mother sign me up for soccer *and* gymnastics *and* piano *and* Girl Scouts, and when I have a goal in any of them, I keep on working until I achieve it. Like in soccer this year? I wanted to be high scorer in at least three games, and I *was*. And in gymnastics—"

Amy knew she'd hear about the girl's successes in gymnastics *and* piano *and* Girl Scouts if she didn't cut her off, so she gave her a big apologetic smile and called out, "Next!"

Next was Isaiah. Amy hated taking his 200 minis after he had given so much money away, but before she could protest, Violet had it safely stashed in their cash box.

Because it felt like cheating to analyze the handwriting of someone she knew so well, Amy let Violet do Isaiah's.

"The spacing between your lines is very narrow. That means . . ." Violet still had to consult her notes sometimes. "It means you're impulsive. You live for the moment. You go for your gut reactions.

"Your right margin is narrow. That means you're racing toward the future. The right margin means the future. And your writing slopes up. See how the line kind of creeps upward?"

The opposite of Todd's, Amy thought.

"That means you're optimistic."

And Todd had said handwriting analysis was bogus!

Half an hour later, Amy and Violet's line was still longer than anyone else's. That was partly because it took a few minutes to analyze someone's writing, even with two people doing it, while it took only a few seconds to hand someone a crayon chicken. But it was mainly because people were fascinated to learn what their handwriting revealed about them.

Their booth had even attracted an audience, because it was also fascinating to learn about other people. Whenever a cute boy showed up for an analysis, several girls would gather around to hear what Amy and Violet had to say. Once Amy caught a glimpse of a pink Frizzy Fred wig in the crowd, but she couldn't tell if it belonged to Julia or Kelsey.

Ms. Ives came for her turn and carefully copied the sample of writing the girls had provided. It was easier to do the analysis if everyone wrote the same few lines with the same kind of pen.

"Should I be nervous?" Ms. Ives asked, sounding nervous.

"No," Violet said. "If we see something really bad, we don't say it."

"That isn't exactly reassuring," Ms. Ives said. "Now I'm going to wonder what really bad thing you saw that you decided not to tell me about."

But Amy didn't see any bad things jumping out from Ms. Ives's sample.

"Your line spacing is clear," she told Ms. Ives. "That means you think clearly and have a sense of order and an ability to plan ahead."

"So far so good," Ms. Ives said.

"Your letters are very connected. That means you pay attention to detail and tend to finish what you start."

"This is getting better and better!"

"Your slant . . ." Amy stopped.

"Oh, no! Is this the really bad thing you're not supposed to tell me about?"

"No, but . . ."

If it was scary being analyzed, it was even scarier doing the analysis, at least when you had to analyze your teacher.

Ms. Ives peered at her own slant. "It's sort of all over the place, isn't it? Usually it slants to the right, but sometimes it slants to the left. What does that mean?"

"It means you're indecisive," Violet put in, helping Amy out. "Variable slant means indecisiveness."

Ms. Ives burst out laughing: "You have me there, girls! I'd be willing to bet that every first-time teacher has variable slant in her writing. I'm just glad I didn't let you analyze my writing six weeks ago, that's all I can say."

Then Ms. Ives turned serious. "We've had a lot of surprises this year, haven't we? That's one thing I think I'm going to be able to count on as a teacher: my students are always going to surprise me."

. . .

When Amy examined Damon's sample a few customers later, her heart sank. Lots of things in it were bad, except that he didn't cross his *t*'s in the strange way that would have suggested he was a serial killer.

Amy shot Violet a warning look. It would be just like Violet to check her notes one more time and then tell him all those things, explaining each character flaw to him patiently, so he'd see the evidence on the paper that pointed to it.

"I'll do this one," Amy said. "How are the calendars selling?" she asked Damon first, to stall for time while she tried to think of what to say.

"You're not going to believe this," he said in a low voice. "They're a bust! Even the parents aren't buying them. I think the problem is that I had to take all the photos the same week, so there's no seasonal variation. People expect a December or January photo to have snow in it. And for April or May they expect a flowering tree. All of mine look like September."

He forced a laugh. "Your brother was smart to go with Crayon Critters. You can tell him I said so."

Poor Damon! Amy had never thought the day would come when she would feel sorry for him, but it had. Failed calendars were obviously every bit as painful as failed pinecones.

"So what does my handwriting say about me?" he asked.

Amy tried to tell him the truth in a positive way. "Um— your lines are, like, *really* regular and neat. That means you're super-organized, but you might want to try loosening up a bit. The loops on your *l*'s are *really* narrow. That means—well, they're not real open-looking, if you see what I mean? You might—well, you don't want to be too open, but maybe a little bit open. Like, to new ideas, and things like that. And the way you connect your letters—some people do it in a rounded way, but you do it in an angular way."

"What does angular show?"

"You're active and assertive."

"That sounds right."

"But maybe too assertive. Sometimes. Like, maybe sometimes you come on a little bit strong?"

Amy couldn't tell from Damon's face what he was thinking.

"So, that'll be two hundred minis."

Damon reached into his pocket and pulled out a crumpled hundred-mini bill. "I was sure I had two hundred minis here. You wouldn't let me give you a calendar for the rest, would you?"

"Sure," Amy agreed, relieved that he didn't seem upset.

For 100 minis plus a Riverside Elementary School calendar, featuring twelve photos of the school in September, Damon had gotten his handwriting analyzed, plus some good advice. It sounded like a terrific deal to Amy.

. . .

Amy hadn't expected Julia and Kelsey to come to the booth as customers, but they did, toward the very end. It was obviously impossible for them to resist.

Should Amy let Violet do their readings, for the same reason she had let Violet do Isaiah's?

No.

"Can you do us together?" Kelsey asked. "Where we just write two lines each?"

"We sort of spent all our money at other booths," Julia said.

"We couldn't stop buying Crayon Critters. Julia thinks Isaiah's assistant is very cute."

"Me? *You're* the one who thinks Todd is so cute. *I* think the Crayon Critters are so cute."

Amy felt a lump coming into her throat. They were chatting with her like old times. Well, not *with* her, exactly, but *near* her. Evidently it was all right to be partners with crybaby Violet if you ended up having the coolest booth in the class. Maybe the long line in front of their booth all afternoon was even enough to make up for having a strange, unemployed dad. Though Amy's dad might not be so strange and unemployed anymore. He had actually made up a flyer for the catering business and mailed it out to all their friends and neighbors.

"Okay," Amy said. "We can do you both together."

She started out telling them what she actually saw. "Your connections between letters are very rounded, for both of you." It was the same feature that had been so angular on Damon's. "That's a very feminine trait."

Julia and Kelsey giggled appreciatively.

"Rounded connections show you want to please other people. And the strong right slant that both of you have shows you're sociable and affectionate. The circles for the dots in your *i*'s—see how you both dot your *i*'s the same way? That means you try to stand out from the crowd, but you also need acceptance."

So much for what she actually saw in the writing. Now she was going beyond what the handwriting books had said: "That means that sometimes you want acceptance *so* much that you get afraid. Of not being accepted. Like, if one of your friends started hanging out with someone unpopular, or had something different happening in her family, you might decide to drop her so that people wouldn't think you were unpopular or different, too."

Kelsey looked up suspiciously. "Does it really mean that?"

"Well, handwriting analysis is more of an art than a science," Amy said, quoting from one of the books. "I'm just telling you what I see. Another analyst might see something else there. Violet, what do you think?"

In a small voice, Violet said, "I see the same things Amy sees."

"Oh," Julia said, still studying her sample.

"So," Kelsey said awkwardly, "do you want to do something with us after school? Like, come to my house and listen to some CDs?"

"I already told Violet I was doing something with her." That wasn't strictly true, but Violet's face brightened. They really *had* become friends.

Julia and Kelsey exchanged glances. "Violet can come, too," Julia said.

"We can't today," Amy said. "But maybe some other time."

And she meant it. She'd be willing to give Julia and Kelsey another chance to be her friends. If the last few weeks had taught Amy anything, they had taught her the importance of second chances.

As Violet counted up their money, Amy sat thinking. Finally she said to Violet, "Do you think handwriting analysis is fake?"

"Wait. Four thousand five hundred. Four thousand six hundred. Four thousand seven hundred. We made four thousand seven hundred minis. And since we had no expenses for materials or anything, it's all profit. Four thousand seven hundred minis!"

"That's great." But Amy didn't really care about the money. Not anymore. "So, do you? Think handwriting analysis is for real? Todd thinks it's fake."

"Ms. Ives *is* indecisive," Violet pointed out.

"But not as much as she used to be."

"Damon *is* a big know-it-all."

"But he admitted that his calendars were a failure, and he didn't try to blame it on anyone but himself."

"You *are* poetic, just like your capital *A* showed. That was the first handwriting analysis I ever did, before we had even read the books."

"Yes, but Todd's capital *T* is the most unpoetic thing you ever saw, and he won the poetry contest, not me." It still hurt, but not as much as it had. Amy had always known that down deep, Todd was more sensitive and poetic than anyone realized—even Todd himself.

"You know what I think?" Amy asked.

"What?"

"I think people are complicated."

Violet waited for a moment, and when Amy didn't elaborate, she said, "That's it? People are complicated?"

"Uh-huh," Amy said. "That's what I think."

Across the room, Amy saw Todd counting the money he and Isaiah had made on Crayon Critters. Of course he would be the one to count the money, not Isaiah.

Amy caught Todd's eye, and they both grinned.